Mahabharat's Stories

Seema Bharti

Become
Shakespeare
.com

First published in 2018 by

Becomeshakespeare.com

Wordit Content Design & Editing Services Pvt Ltd
Unit - 26, Building A -1, Nr Wadala RTO,
Wadala (East), Mumbai 400037, India
T: +91 8080226699

Wordit Art Fund helps deserving authors publish their work by providing
monetary support. To apply for funding, please visit us at
www.BecomeShakespeare.com

ISBN - 978-93-87649-71-2

Disclaimer

This book is a study of the epic, Mahabharat. Some characteristics have been changed, some events have been compressed and some dialogues have been recreated.

About the Author

I studied English literature for my post graduation from Panjab University, India. Literature and philosophy fascinated me. The invaluable works of different authors presented various facets of the great epic, Mahabharat. It inspired me to make my own formulations as to what I feel about the characters and the whole scenario in general.

Table of Contents

CHAPTER 1 - Anukramanika Parva   1

CHAPTER 2 - Parvasamgraha   11

CHAPTER 3 - Poushya Parva   13

CHAPTER 4 - Poulama Parva   20

CHAPTER 5 - Astika Parva   23

CHAPTER 6 - Adi-vamshavatarana   46

CHAPTER 7 - Sambhava Parva   54

CHAPTER 8 - Jatugriha Daha Parva   115

CHAPTER 9 - Hidimba Vadha Parva   128

CHAPTER 10 - Baka Vadha Parva   134

CHAPTER 11 - Chaitraratha Parva   140

CHAPTER 12 - Draupadi Svayamvara Parva   155

CHAPTER 13 - Vaivahika Parva   163

CHAPTER 14 - Viduragama   167

CHAPTER 15 - Rajya Labha   173

CHAPTER 16 - Arjuna Vanavasa Parva   175

CHAPTER 17 - Subhadra-Harana Parva   182

CHAPTER 18 - Harana Harika Parva   185

CHAPTER 19 - Khandava Daha Parva   188

CHAPTER 20 - Sabha Parva   194

PREFACE

Mahabharat is the longest epic written till date. Like the Greek heroes, it is full of valiant warriors who are capable of moving mountains but get entangled in personal and emotional turmoil leading to their defeat. This work, Mahabharat's Stories, present a realistic view of the centuries old epic, which is in alignment with today's struggles and hardships.

The protagonists Kauravs and Pandavs are doomed by destiny right from birth. Unfortunately, they are cousins and happen to cross paths at every turn of life that culminates into the pivotal battle of Kurukshetra. Nothing succeeds like success. Kauravs lost in the battle. They were the bad boys, the villains of the piece. But was Dhritrashtra, the father of Kauravs, a perpetrator of evil or was wronged himself! Lawfully, the kingdom belonged to him, in keeping with the law of inheritance, but went to his younger brother Pandu, for reasons beyond him. Also, Duryodhana the son, has been referred to as Suyodhana. Both are epitaphs for malevolence and great warriors. Then why is he always depicted as evil incarnate!

Mahabharat represents a primitive society. There is fight over cattle and land but at the same time it talks of flying chariots like our airplanes and weapons of mass destruction. It is absolutely live. It is littered with real life places thriving even today in India. The epic deals with everyday issues like infertility, death, surrogacy, greed, revenge, inheritance and celibacy. Political alliances forged through marriages helped to fight warring enemies and neighbors.

In Mahabharat, it is difficult to decide, between good and bad and still more who is evil and otherwise. The good ones have their moments of baseness and the so-called evil of magnanimity. Good and bad are in continuation, only varying in degrees and not two different entities. Throughout the epic, the characters face a conflict of interests, duty versus morality! As human beings, we face this dilemma in our everyday lives. Hence Mahabharat becomes humane and the reader can relate to it. There are no absolute answers. Depending on our choices, we face the consequence.

CHAPTER ONE
Anukramanika Parva

AN OVERVIEW

Once Ugrashrava visited a boarding school in a forest. The pupil there were holding a felicitation ceremony for Professor Shounaka. They gathered around Ugrashrava. They wanted to hear from him, his wonderful stories. Ugrashrava, was a charioteer and bard by profession. His father was a warrior but mother was a teacher. Most royal charioteers were bards. They had deep knowledge of literature and philosophy.

Ugrashrava had been to the Naga sacrifice wherein all the Nagas, the forest dwellers would be eliminated by Janemajaya to avenge the death of his father Parikshit. Parikshit was killed by the Naga king, Takshaka. Vaishampayana, Krishna Dvaipayana's disciple was also present. There he narrated the diverse stories composed by his master. Ugrashrava was overwhelmed. He visited Samantapachaka, where the battle between the cousins Kauravs and Pandavs had taken place.

Mahabharat is the history of kings, warriors, teachers and their pupil and has essence of all philosophical texts beautiful in language with subtle meanings and logic. It is a great storehouse of knowledge adorned with words and rhyme. With the evolution of the universe, evolved the inexhaustible seeds of all its inhabitants, movable and immovable, water, earth, wind, years and seasons. All came into existence.

Without beginning and end, the wheel of existence moves on eternally, wherein one era decays and simultaneously another arises. Thus with evolution arose the Brahma, the self created universe.

From the Brahma arose, lineage of scholars, a class of them getting royal patronage, teachers residing in forests and householders. Kurus, Yadus and the Bharatas descended from the lines of Yayati, Ikshvaku and all the royal teachers.

Satyavati's son Krishna Dvaipayna composed the Mahabharat. The text is a large storehouse of classified verses, intermingled with the rules of conduct for the world, mainly duties, making wealth and being prosperous, worldly desires and release after the cycle of death.

It also has ancient history of kings, knowledge of Yoga wherein human soul unites with the universe and knowledge obtained through self realization and the revelations heard and passed on down the ages.

Krishna Dvaipyna, the learned scholar, after gruelling hard work, classified the verses and composed them. On the request of his mother Satyavati, he agreed to be the father to step-brother Vichitravirya's sons. Thus were born Dhritarashtra, Pandu and Vidhur. Having done his duty, he returned to his hermitage, to old life of austerities and continued his work on the Mahabharat and other texts.

After his sons had passed on their supreme journey, he revealed the Mahabharat to the world. On the insistence of Janemajaya, his disciple Vaishampayna, recited the Mahabharat at the Naga sacrifice organised by Janemajaya to the assembly of teachers and scholars, gathered there.

Krishna Dvaipayna first taught this epic to his son Shuka and later to his disciples. According to him, among the Kauravs, Duryodhan was image incarnate of passion and anger, Karna his right hand, Shakuni his mind, Duhshashana his split image, and father Dhritarashtra the roots, with no sense of direction and authority.

In the Pandava clan, Yudhisthira was the righteous one, Bhim symbol of strength, Arjun the trunk, Nakul and Sahdev the good and obedient, Krishna and their teachers the roots.

Pandu, retired to the forests, after waging many wars and battles. One day while hunting, he killed Kindama while he was mating with his wife. Pandu's guilt and evil deeds took his life. Thus, Pandu's sons were born from the different wise, learned men epitomising qualities of Duty, Strength and Power. The Pandavs were born and brought up in the forest under the care of mothers Kunti and Madri, in the company of wise, learned men.

When the boys were old enough, they took them to Dhrithrashtra and introduced to him, his brother Pandu's sons. There were voices of dissent. How could Pandavs be Pandu's sons! He had died long ago, they wondered! But in general, the people of the city welcomed them wholeheartedly.

The Pandavs, had been born and brought up in the forest, in the company of sagacious ones, and had spent time studying the art of warfare and philosophy. They were respected by all.

Arjuna got the hand of Draupadi, in marriage, owing to his skills as a world class archer; an unparalleled warrior. Yudhisthira performed the Coronation ceremony with the help of his brothers Arjuna, Bhim, Nakul and Sahdev, and the able advice of Krishna. He subjugated warring kings and princes. This gave him the right to Coronation ceremony, rich in provision, sacrifices and merit. At the time of

Coronation ceremony, other kings and princes accept the superiority of the crowned monarch and pay him rich tributes.

Duryodhan also came to the Coronation ceremony. The prosperity and power of the Pandavs, made him angry and envious. His evil mind started working. With the help of his uncle Shakuni, who was a magician at the game of dice, he challenged the Pandavs. Being a warrior, Yudhisthira accepted the challenge, despite not being good at the game. Destiny takes its course. Even with the presence of magnificent warriors and wise men, Krishna, Vidhur, Bhishma, Drona, and Kripa the war between the cousins Kauravs and Pandavs followed.

The news of the victory of Pandavas, in the battle of Kurukshetra, by Sanjaya, his charioteer, puts Dhritarashtra in a mood of retrospection. Lacking emotional vision, he conveniently laid the blame on his sons. He poured out his heart. Thus he lamented. "Sanjaya, I was frustrated and disappointed with life. But I loved my sons immensely. I was helpless because of my old age and blind state. I could not stand up to their follies because I loved them and that weakened me. My sons in turn were upset with me because of my incapacity.

Duryodhan saw the wealth and power of Pandavs at the Coronation ceremony. He was also mocked for his ignorance. This made him angry and envious. Like a warrior he could not match their skill in the battle field and be prosperous. So he planned an unfair game of dice with a wrong ally. I had a premonition of things to come. I may not able to see but I have vision.

Arjun had shown the world, that he was the best archer, the Sun, in the field of battle. Thus he got the hand of Draupadi in marriage. I saw no ray of hope for Duryodhana and his brothers then. Yudhisthira and his brothers had been defeated in an unfair game of dice by Shakuni and deprived of their kingdom. I sensed a fierce hurricane in the future coming for Duryodhana and his brothers.

Arjun married Subhadra in Dwarka and was accompanied by her brothers Vasudev Krishna and Balram to Indraprastha. As a result, the Pandavas had powerful allies. Fortune was favouring the Pandavas. Krishna helped Arjuna burn down the Khandava forest and made it their abode.

After the game of dice, Draupadi was dragged to the assembly hall, in tears, in the presence of all the elders of the family and her brave husbands. I knew she would be avenged and no one would be able to stop the Pandavas.

The humiliated, righteous Pandavas left for the forest, after losing in an unfair game of dice. Deep down I knew wrongdoers would be punished. Thousands of learned men celibate and about to initiate domestic life, followed Yudhisthira to the forest. Pandavas had the company and blessings of so many wise people.

Arjuna after lots of penance, austerities and gruelling hard work, received the Pashupata weapon, the weapon of mass destruction. After lots of inhuman efforts, the boy received deadly weapons. He learnt to use them too. Duryodhan and his brothers' defeat was destined.

O Sanjaya, my foolish sons, on Karna's advice, went on a cattle related expedition and got captured by the folk singers and were freed by Arjuna. Yudhisthira, even in the face of death, enacted according to laws of Duty, reinforcing his magnanimous character. Arjuna lived in disguise in the kingdom of Virata. Even then he defeated my best, Duryodhan, in combat.

Virata, the king of Matsya, with great honour offered his daughter Uttara to Arjun in marriage for his son Abhimanyu. The Pandavs thus had one more powerful ally.

Yudhisthira, without wealth or a kingdom, had managed to raise a huge army. He had no friends or relatives; was in exile, in disguise. Without a kingdom, Yudhisthira had all the qualities of a king, just, brave, and strong. The intelligent learned Narada had visualized Krishna and Arjun, as warriors, the wise ones. Duryodhan and his brothers did not stand a chance.

The Pandavs had the patronage of Krishna, who had defeated the strong, evil king Bali, once. Duryodhan and Karna had once, on purpose tried to insult Krishna in the presence of the whole assembly. Krishna, wise that he was, showed his true colours, strength, character, fearlessness and power.

O Sanjaya, Krishna has lots of love and affection for his aunt Kunti. He would never let her down. Krishna has become advisor to Bhishma, my powerful brother, and Dronacharya in turn, has blessed Krishna.

Duryodhan and his forces were divided right at the very beginning. Bhishma and Karna the two pillars disagreed and decided not to fight as long as the other was fighting. How would Duryodhan win, when doyens, Krishna and Arjun and the fiery weapon Gandhiva came together! All three of non combustible energy.

In the course of the battle Arjuna was overcome by self doubt. Krishna successfully counselled him. Arjun regained his lost vision and foresight. Victory seemed to dodge the Kauravas. Bhishma, the brave and fearsome warrior killed plentiful of the enemy camp but failed to kill anyone noteworthy.

Arjun conquered the Bhishma of infinite courage by placing Shikandi before him. Bhishma, the unconquerable laid on a bed of arrows wounded by a single arrow. On the battlefield Arjuna displaying his human side and slaked Bhishma's thirst while he was on the bed of arrows. Even the Universe helped them in their victory.

Dronacharya, the most skilled teacher, displayed and used many weapons but failed to kill any Pandav. Warriors of highest rank, the ones who never leave the battlefield without killing were deployed to kill Arjun but they all were in turn banished by him.

Arjun's son Abhimanyu single handed penetrated our war formation, impenetrable and guarded by Dronacharya. Unable to kill Arjun, our warriors collectively gathered and pounded on his son instead and rejoiced at his death. Furious Arjun vowed revenge on King Jayadratha, on hearing that Dhrithrashtra and his cruel sons cheered at his son's death. Arjun kept his vow and killed Jayadratha.

Krishna, a great warrior himself, unyoked Arjun's horses, gave them water and yoked them back when they were exhausted, like a true charioteer. Karna, the brave warrior, merely abused Bhim of immense strength but did not kill him. Arjun kept enemy at bay with his arrow Gandiva when his horses were exhausted. Satyaki, created chaos in Dronacharya's army with his elephant of unmatched strength and returned unharmed to Krishna and Arjun.

King Jayadrath was killed by the enemy despite the presence of great warriors Dronacharya, Asvhvathamma, Karna, Kripacharya and king Shalya. Karna's spear, a weapon of unmatched potential and highly destructive, could have killed Arjun but failed to do so. When aimed at Arjun, Krishna sank the chariot low and instead it killed Ghatotchaka, Bhim's son. The spear that could have killed the mighty Arjun, was unleashed by the son of a charioteer, Karna.

Dhrishtadyumna, violated all norms of battle and killed Drona, when he was in no position to fight back. Nakula, got into a chariot duel with son of Drona, Ashvathamma, a fearsome warrior and proved himself to be his equal. Ashvathamma, used the weapon Narayana, of supreme unmatchable strength but failed to kill any Pandav.

It is beyond comprehension that how could Karna, a fearsome, unconquerable warrior be killed by Arjun. Victory seemed to betray us, as Ashvathamma, Dushassana, Kritavarma, all fearsome warriors, collectively failed to defeat Arjuna. Yudhisthira killed Shalya, King of Madra, who always belittled Krishna. Pandav Sahdev, killed the evil Shakuni, who had orchestrated the entire quarrel.

I lost all hope of victory, when Duryodhan lay defeated in a pond of water, without his chariot, tired, defeated, stripped of self respect and pride. The Pandavs accompanied by Krishna insulted my son. In the battle of clubs that ensued, despite of having displayed, exceptional valour and skill, he was unjustly killed on the advice of Krishna.

Drona's son Ashwathamma, performed an unforgivable ghastly act, by killing Draupadi's sons while they were asleep. Ashvathamma, aimed the mighty weapon Aishika, at Abhimanyu's unborn child in Uttara's womb in anger when pursued by Bhim.

O Sanjaya, there was no respite from attacks and counter attacks. Ashvathamma released a deadly weapon Brahmashira. Arjun neutralized it with another deadly weapon. But for this debacle, Ashvathamma had to sacrifice the jewel of his head and that was humiliating.

O' my wife Gandhari is suffering, in agony. She has lost her sons, brothers, father, and grandsons in this war. Only ten warriors have survived the war. Only ten! There were eighteen armies of warriors. The Pandavs now have the throne without a rival. There is no hope but only darkness around me. I feel emotionally defeated and drained out".

Misery, sorrow and hopelessness of death and defeat of his sons and army completely defeated Dhrithrashtra and his purpose of life. He no longer had the will to live. Sanjaya, with his wise thoughts and words, enlightened the dejected and dispirited king about the fate of men. He recounted the stories, as told by Dvaipayna and Narada.

"There were men born in royal families. Some were great warriors, adept at the use of fearsome and destructive weapons. They were as good as, Gods of war. Their moral values were above board, performed lots of sacrifices, shone brightly on earth, completed their journey and left to reach their final abode. They had great strength, did not hesitate to take on their enemy to the extent finished them and were the bearers of good deeds. Vishwamitra, Rama the son of Dashratha and Yayati are just a few stars in the constellation.

Shaivya, was devastated at the loss of his son. Narada, quoted to him twenty four others, who had been through this journey of misery. Shaivya was not alone in this cycle.

There were good men, who gave up worldly pleasures and wealth, were powerful and wise but had to don the garb of death. Great souls fortified with truth, purity, simplicity, righteousness, great riches, some with abundant faith and simplicity left for heavenly abode."

"Dhrithrashtra, have no misconceptions. Your sons were cruel, greedy and mean. Between good and evil, they choose evil. Do not feel sorry for them. You are a learned man. You have vast knowledge of Philosophy and warfare. Your emotions have always had control over your mind. You protected your sons no matter how evil their actions!

No one can escape fate. You are an intelligent and wise man. Do not get carried away by false notions and beliefs. There is no point grieving about something that was bound to happen. Everything is preordained. A wise man does not lament at misfortunes or rejoice in fortunes. No one can ever change the path laid out by time.

Time is supreme. It has no rivals. It keeps moving even when we stop and rest. Time is the creator and the destroyer of all beings. Past, present and future is the creation of time, wherein human beings have no role to play. So why be unhappy where there is no role for one to play. Time burns the heart, but it douses the fire too. It is the creator of happiness, sadness, evil and goodness. It pervades all aspects of life, living and nonliving but is impartial. It dictates terms. Your sons were greedy, envious and driven by passion. Their fate was inevitable. So do not be sorrowful".

Dvaipayna created Mahabharat. People who read it and understand the meaning, achieve wisdom. It is full of valorous deeds of learned men and warriors. Krishna has been immortalised. He is the personification of truth, valour and strength. He shall live down the ages through his teachings in his philosophical discourse, the Bhagvad Gita.

The self created universe is the father, God. From the universe arises the living and the non living. It takes the form of five elements, earth, water, energy, wind, sky and three qualities namely creation, preservation and destruction.

Mahabharat is rich in content and substance. Knowledge, austerities, spending time reading of history, philosophy, science, maths, the art of warfare, to the extent pursuits in making money is not a sin. These become evil and sinful when they are used to abuse others.

CHAPTER TWO
Parvasamgraha

THE HISTORY OF THE BATTLEGROUND

The pupil at the felicitation ceremony of Shounaka, gathered around Ugrashrava, the bard. They urged him to describe the holy place of Samantapanchaka, which he had visited before coming. Thus began Ugrashrava, "At the juncture of Treta and Dvapara era, Parasurama, the great scholar warrior, created five lakes at Samantapanchaka. He was angered at the atrocities committed by the King's soldiers. Thus began their decimation. He offered their blood to his ancestors. His anger and rage was beyond control.

Once in his agitated state of mind, while asleep, his paternal grandfather Richika apparently appeared before him and requested him to be calm and stop the killings. Heeding advice, Parashurama instead built five lakes. Thus, the region around these five lakes is called the holy land of Samantapanchaka".

History repeats itself. Again at the juncture of Dvapara and Kali era, a battle was fought to eliminate evil from the equation. The Kauravs and the Pandavas fought this battle at the land of Samantapanchaka. Time and again when evil starts overflowing, someone has to start and stop its journey.

Thus eighteen battalions of warriors assembled at the holy land of Samantapanchaka, to free the earth again from vice. Eighteen battalions can be roughly translated into one lakh, nine thousand, three hundred and fifty soldiers, with the same number of elephants and sixty five thousand, six hundred and ten horses.

Eighteen battalions were all destroyed, in spite of the towering presence of doyens skilled in highest art of warfare. Though Bhishma, Drona, Karna, Shalya and the powerful allies were adept at the art of decimating the enemy still the Kauravs lost. The evil intentions of the Kauravs did not let them win. The cause towered over skill. The sons of Drona, Hardikya and Goutama stooped real low and killed Yudhisthira's soldiers while they were asleep.

CHAPTER THREE
Poushya Parva

NAGA KING TAKSHAKA

Janemajaya, son of Parikshit and great grandson of Arjun, attended a long conference of scholars along with his brothers. Sarameya, the underdog, came wandering to the meet. He was humiliated by Janemajya's brothers. At home, on seeing him sad, his mother Sarama, prodded and asked him the reason. "Mother, for no apparent reason, I was embarrassed. I was stopped at the entrance and not allowed access. All I wanted was to hear great minds talk", he lamented. Sarama, went mad with fury. In raging anger, she marched up to Janemajaya, where he was attending the meet.

"Janemajaya", she said, "My son did no wrong. Still you denied him entry. Evil shall befall on you when you least expect it. Your brothers committed a crime, by hurting an innocent creature, for no fault of his". Shell shocked Janemajaya was extremely remorseful. He wished the incident had not taken place.

Once the sacrifice was over, Janemajaya returned to Hastinapur. He set out in search of a learned tutor, who would counteract the effects of the wrongs done and teach right conduct. One day Janemajaya, went out for a hunt. He came across a residential school, at a lonely place in his kingdom. There professor Shrutashrava lived with his son Somashrava.

Wishing to make Somashrava his tutor, Janemajaya requested the father."Janemajaya" said Shrutashrava, "my son is endowed with great knowledge and learning. He is a great scholar. He can absolve you of all your shortcomings but he has his own limitations. He can never refuse another ascetic anything he asks for". Janemajaya readily agreed. He accepted Somashrava as his mentor and returned.

He instructed his brothers thus."Somashrava, from now onwards, would be our teacher. Obey his teachings and instructions, unquestioningly". The brothers agreed. He, himself then started his march against the kingdom of Takshila and brought it under control.

During that period, there was another renowned professor Ayoda-Dhoumya. He had three disciples Upamanyu, Aruni and Veda. One day, the preceptor assigned the task of stopping a breach in the dike to his disciple Aruni. Aruni readily agreed. He immediately left. He could not find any means of plugging the breach.

Suddenly, an idea flashed across his mind. He himself entered the breach and laid down there. The water flow stopped. After some time, Ayoda Dhoumya and other disciples on not seeing Aruni around, went in search of him. Ayoda called out for Aruni aloud. Hearing the voice of the preceptor, Aruni arose from the breach and appeared before him. "Sir, I was in the breach in the dike, to stop the flow of water. There was no other way the breach could be mended" thus explained Aruni.

The preceptor was over joyous. His disciple had successfully conducted the task, assigned to him. He was learning well. Ayoda blessed him, "Son, let all the learnings of philosophical texts be bestowed on you. Let good fortune be your companion. From now on you shall be called Uddalaka, since you have opened the flow of water by standing up from the breach in the dike".

Ayoda, then assigned a task to his second pupil, Upmanyu. He was asked to look after the cows. Ayoda found Upmanyu, overfed and healthy. He asked him about his means of sustenance. "After, looking after the cows, I go out and beg. I live on alms", said Upamanyu. Ayoda reprimanded, "One should not be covetous. But instead, share everything with others and at the same time not take others means of sustenance, even if they give it, out of generosity".

Henceforth, Upamanyu, started giving away everything he acquired from cow's milk and even the leftovers to his preceptor. Thus having practically nothing to eat one day, Upmanyu, ended up eating leaves of arka plant to quench his hunger. Meanwhile Ayoda, on not seeing Upmanyu around, assumed that the boy must have been hungry and angry, hence had not returned. He went out in search of him and cried out aloud.

Upamanyu, called back, saying he had fallen in a well, after eating leaves of the arka plant, that turned him blind. Ayoda, asked him to pray to the self created universe, who is the mentor of all on earth.

Upamanyu prayed thus, "Oh Brahma! You were born even before anyone else came into existence. You are all pervading. Your presence is manifested in all beings, living and nonliving. You are free from all falsehood and decay. O' Creators of Sun, Creator of day and night, rescuer of life from the clutches of time! You are the creator of ten directions including zenith and nadir. You placed the sun and moon above. Humans sleep and wake up, in alignment with courses of sun and moon. O' Brahma! You are the seed of everything. After mixing many colours you have created a wonderful feast for the eyes, from which were created earth, universe and sky. You are the male, the female, everything present on this earth, living and dead. Yet you have no form. You are omnipotent. Kindly restore my eyesight."

Everyone present was astounded by his knowledge and learning. He credited all the wisdom to his preceptor, as he was the man behind the enlightened individual that he was today. The people present blessed him with good sight and good fortune. In the meantime, the acrid effect of the arka leaves subsided. He could see again. Upamanyu profoundly thanked his preceptor and took leave.

Ayoda, assigned an apparently simple task to his disciple Veda. He was to stay in his preceptor's house and obey all his orders without questioning him. Obediently, Veda toiled day and night without complaining, bore extreme heat and cold patiently, at times even went to bed without food. Ayoda, pleased with Veda's obedience, hard work and sincerity blessed him with good fortune and complete knowledge and bid him farewell.

Veda embarked on a journey of being a householder. Veda refrained from being severe on his disciples, two young warriors Poushya and Janemajaya, as he had suffered lots of hardships and miseries in his preceptor's house.

Veda also had a disciple Utanka. One day, he called him and said, "Utanka, my son, I have to go on a long journey. Look after the house and its members as would deem appropriate ". He followed the preceptor's instructions diligently.

Once the women of the house gathered around him and requested him to impregnate the Veda's wife, as it was the right time of the month. Without a second thought he refused. He felt it improper. Veda felt extremely happy on learning this. As a teacher he had fulfilled his duty. His disciple did not succumb to temptation and did what was righteous. Utanka got Veda's blessings and permission to leave. Instead, Utanka asked Veda to allow him to pay back the debt incurred. He said, "We have to be grateful and gracious enough to reciprocate the good, one does to us or else we shall be sinned against". However, not wanting to disappoint his disciple he passed on the onus to his wife. His wife wanted Utanka to get her King Poushya's wife's earrings. She wanted them within four days, to look radiant at the time of serving her guests.

Utanka left to fulfill Veda's wife's wish. On the way he came across a giant sized man, with an equally large bull. He offered Utanka some unsavoury looking food to eat. Utanka initially refused, but on learning that his preceptor too had eaten the same food, he immediately accepted. The very mention of his preceptor cleansed his mind of all doubts. An old, wise man Parajayna and his horse Agni, on seeing the youth, offered him nectar, blessing him with a long happy life. Utanka moved on and reached King Poushya's kingdom. The king and Utanka greeted each other respectfully. Utanka told Poushya the purpose of his visit. "Go in to my wife's chamber and ask for her earrings but make sure you are pure both physically and emotionally. Have no evil intentions.", he instructed.

On entering the Queen's chamber, Utanka requested her to give him her earrings. The queen was taken in by Utanka's honest and straightforward talk. She immediately handed over her earrings but warned against Takshaka, the Naga king who was also after them. Utanka profusely thanked the Queen and asked for leave.

Poushya requested Utanka to stay back for some time as he wished to make holy offerings to his ancestors, and a man of Utanka's stature would be the best person. Utanka, wanted to reach his preceptor's wife on time and time was running out. But he agreed grudgingly. To add to the confusion, he found the cook's hair in the food. The young man in an already agitated state of mind accused the king of being disrespectful. Poushya reciprocated the feelings with equal anger as he never intended to insult the boy. Both of them finally relented, realising that nothing was concurred intentionally. Being a warrior Poushya found it hard to forgive, for a warrior's words are soft but heart is hard unlike that of a learned man. But no evil resulted from the incident.

On his way to his preceptor's house, Utanka came across the Naga king Takshaka, who appeared dressed as a mendicant. Unsuspectingly, he placed the earrings on the ground and went to quench his thirst. Takshaka, disappeared with the earrings. But Utanka was not the one to give up. He followed Takshaka right up to his kingdom."Oh! King Takshaka, inhabitant of Kurukshetra and Khandva region! I humbly salute you. You and your subjects adorn battlefields and charge on the enemy like lightning. Oh! Subjects of Airavrata you shine like the sun in the sky. No one in the army would like to march in the blazing sun without you".

Utanka, still did not get the earrings. He did not give up. He implored, "Creator of this universe! Creator of day and night, protector of this universe and destroyer of demons! Bearer of truth and lies, please help me! Let the Nagas be in my power.

Ultimately not able to make Takshaka see reason, he burnt down the kingdom of Nagas. Takshaka ran out in fear, handing over the earrings to Utanka. After giving the earrings to his preceptor's wife and seeking blessings and permission to leave, Utanka went towards Hastinapur.

King Janemajaya had just arrived, after a victorious battle in Takshila and was celebrating it with his advisors. The king greeted Utanka respectfully, "Janemajaya, do not waste your time, rejoicing in these achievements. Your life has a greater purpose", said Utanka. The king was confused. He was an honest warrior and looked after his subjects well. What was the learned one hinting at, he wondered!

Utanka was angry with Takshaka. He wanted a great warrior like Janemajaya to settle scores with him. Utanka explained, "Your father was killed by Takshaka. He was a noble soul. Takshaka, high on power, never realised his folly. Do the necessary to avenge your father and me." Utanka's words infuriated the king. The king consulted his advisors and asked them for details of his father's journey to death. He was overcome with grief and sorrow.

CHAPTER FOUR
Poulama Parva

THE NAGA VENOM

Professor Shounaka, was the descendant of Brighu lineage. He was keen on learning stories of his ancestors. Thus spoke Ugrashrava, "Your great grandfather Brighu had a lovely wife Puloma. She was an epitome of beauty. Both of them were on way to parenthood. During that period, in Brighu's absence, the evil Puloman came to their humble dwelling. Puloma served the guest well".

Unfortunately, for the lady, Puloman was filled with lust on seeing her beauty. In the presence of purifying, Fire, under duress, Puloma confessed, "I am the same woman, who was betrothed to you, before marriage to Brighu. On seeing your evil ways, my father changed his mind and gave my hand to the learned ascetic ". Puloma could not lie, even in an attempt to save herself, from the demon, in the presence of Fire, a symbol of righteousness and purity!

Anyone who knows the truth about an action but knowingly does not speak up, is sure to be tainted by sin! "Since, I was to marry this beautiful woman and Brighu deceitfully took her away, she is mine!" Mentally justified the demon. He then carried Puloma forcibly, with him.

With the force and violence around her, the son in her womb, began to writhe in pain. He simply wished to perish. Puloma too began to convulse in pain. The demon's senses revolted. He saw the agony of the mother and the unborn child. He almost died in grief, leaving them behind for she was not the beautiful woman he was once betrothed to. She was someone's wife and mother. In spite of the odds, Brighu's strong son Chyavana came to life.

Brighu's heart burst with anger at the atrocities suffered by his wife and son due to Fire's righteousness, at the hands of evil Puloman. The purifying Fire had been unjust to him, his innocent wife and unborn child. "Mankind shall no longer have faith in Fire", fumed the sage in anger. In future, it shall be a mute witness to both good and evil in this world. It shall be the mouth to the food served to the departed ancestors and Gods, and at the same time it shall be a witness to the lies.

Chyavana, had a son Pramati from his wife Sukanya. Pramati had a son Ruru from Ghritachi and Shounaka from wife Pramadvara. Pramadvara, was the daughter of great beauty Menaka and King Vishvavasm. The king had refused to owe up the child. Menaka thus delivered the child near Sage Sthulakesha's hermitage on the banks of the river and left. Taken in by the girl's angelic innocence and beauty, the sage adopted her as her own and named her Pramadvara, one of unsurpassable beauty and qualities.

One day Ruru, happened to pass by the hermitage. He saw the divine beauty Pramadvara. He fell in love with her. His father Pramati and Sage Sthulakesha, anointed a day for their marriage. Once, the maiden was out in the forest with her friends, when she accidentally placed her foot on a sleeping Naga on the ground. She was hit so hard with the Naga's venom and anger that she fainted. Ruru, his father and the sage, saw her lying lifeless on the ground. Their hearts were filled with anguish and pain.

Ruru wept in agony, on seeing his beloved almost dead. He fervently prayed to God to bring a smile on her face. Earlier in the day he had, had a strange vision. His beloved was being carried away by Satan. He in turn was begging and holding his feet. Satan after much cajoling agreed on one condition. Ruru would have to give up, half of his life span working for the welfare of the less privileged.

Ruru got up with a start. Even God could not refuse to grant the lovelorn his heartfelt desire, for he had led a life of austerities and was learned. With God's blessings, Pramadvara came back to life. Shortly afterwards both were married. Unfortunately Ruru's heart hardened towards all Nagas. He killed them mindlessly whenever and wherever he saw them.

One day his inner voice commanded him to stop the mindless killing since he did not know which one was evil and which one was not, like the non poisonous snake dunduba. He was committing a grave crime. Why punish someone for a crime he had not committed! He was a teacher and not a warrior. His duty was to follow the path of nonviolence and not take life of any other living creature. According to laws of Nature a teacher was supposed to be always non violent, truthful, forgiving, peaceful and learned. In the past a lot of nagas were sacrificed by Janemajaya. Later, Astika, who was a scholar, brave and strong came to their rescue.

CHAPTER FIVE

Astika Parva

King Janamejaya wanted everyone of Takshaka the Naga King and his race, dead. Takshaka had killed his father Parikshit, out of arrogance and inflated in power and did not even repent. Janamejaya was vying for his blood. The sagacious Astika saved the innocent nagas, and the sinner Takshaka from his rage.

NAGA SISTERS VINATA AND KADRU

During that period there was another naga King Daksha. His daughters Vinata and Kadru were married to the learned Kashyapa. Kadru wished to have lots of sons of unsurpassable energy and was blessed with them. Vinata wished to have only two but greater in strength and energy than her sister's sons. Unfortunately one of her sons Aruna was born deformed and died at the time of birth. Her second son, whom she named Garuda, after the king of birds, was the enemy of the Nagas. Like a true son he delivered his mother from her sister's bondage.

Once both the sisters, Vinata and Kadru spotted Ucchaishrava, a horse, supreme of unsurpassed energy and forever youthful. Ucchaishrava was said to be the horse with wings. It could run very fast in rain, thunderstorm, in the battle field and in raging wars. It had arisen when a tsunami had churned the ocean and its marine and forest life had been uprooted and destroyed.

Gods had consulted each other to find means and ways of obtaining nectar. Vishnu had consulted Brahma. "Churn the ocean, with the help of gods and demons, all the goodness, nectar, real jewels and oil shall emerge", he had advised.

The great mount Mandara, home to fierce animals, melodious birds, soaring peaks, covered with extensive creepers and herbs, experienced flaming winds, lightening, showers, heavy rainfall and thunder. With the whirlwind, trees were uprooted, some of them rubbed against each other producing friction. This led to jungle fires.

The flowers from the trees, rained down with the rain. The fire burnt down its inhabitants, lions, elephants and other creatures, and drove out the living. The entire mountain got uprooted, falling in the ocean, housed on the tortoises' and their king Akupara on their backs. But with the crashing of the mountain, into the ocean marine life almost died, in the underground depth. The snakes twirled the water of the ocean.

On one side was the cloud of smoke, with traces of lightening, arising from the mountain, and on other side was the ocean, churning fiercely like a tsunami in the offing. Seeing enough anger and destruction in the mountain, Lord Indra, the rain god, gently poured. The juices of the herbs, plants, flowers, resins of large trees, flowed into the ocean, creating nectar.

The ocean became calm; the moon arose from the bed of the ocean, with its brilliant rays, casting a spell on the surrounding. A beautiful powerful horse Ucchaishrava was also seen. Invaluable gems and stones, adorned the bed of the ocean. Oil put a protective covering.

The demons got bewitched by the beauty of the calm ocean and the abundance of wealth. They got lost in the fun and frolic. In the meantime the noble started drinking the nectar from the ocean. Seeing this, the demons too started clamouring for it.

Future saw a great battle between the good and the evil for ambrosia. Rahu, the demon was killed in the process and so many others too. Finally nectar was preserved in the hands of the wise.

The Naga sisters' Vinata and Kadru saw the beautiful horse Ucchaishrava. An evil desire came forth in Kadru's mind on seeing the horse. She too wished to be like Ucchaihshrava, supreme. Very cunningly she invited Vinata to have a wager. With the help of her sons, she succeeded in deceiving Vinata and became her overlord. Most of her sons had refused to participate in the game of deception.

"What is the use of sons who would not help their mother realise her dreams. They are as good as dead," she cursed. Humanity cringed at her thoughts. But her curse was a blessing in disguise for the Nagas.

The Nagas had greatly multiplied in number and lots of them were extremely lethal and vicious of excessive strength. They attacked unprovoked. She wished her sons were killed by Janemajaya in the Naga sacrifice. Kadru and Vinata reached the ocean from where Ucchaihshrava had arisen.

The bed of the ocean was full of precious stones, gems and shells. Fierce aquatic animals danced in its waters. Crocodiles, turtles, whales, sharks roared making thunderous sounds. The winds and the courses of sun and moon caused turbulence in the waterbed with the waves dancing everywhere. The ocean had thousand of rivers gushing in to join, making it impossible to locate the river bed. Its holy water quenched Fire's thirst. It was vast and as extended as the sky.

BIRTH OF GARUDA; THE PRODIGAL NAGA SON

In the meantime, Vinata gave birth to her son Garuda of infinite energy. Vinata prayed when her powerful son came into being. "Oh! Son! You are a rishi! You are equal in energy to fire! You are full of strength and purity! You cannot be conquered. You shall perform great acts. You shall destroy everything dark. You shall destroy everything at the end of the Era, which caused destruction. You epitomise the permanent, the transient, and the perishable. Kindly take us in your shadow." Garuda felt humbled by the tributes paid by his mother and the sages.

Vinata lived in bondage on one side of the ocean. Her sister Kadru, made her run errands. One day, she wanted Vinata, to take her to the beautiful abode of the Nagas, in the heart of the ocean. Vinata and Garuda took Kadru and her sons to the island. On the way, the scorching heat of the sun almost burnt the brave ones.

Their mother Kadru, prayed to the Mighty Rain, "Oh! Rain, the powerful and mighty! My sons, the Nagas are dying. Pour your blessings on them! You are Wind! You are the dense clouds. You are the creator, the destroyer. Unconquerable! You are the king! You are time! You are the oceans with mighty whales. Scholars' and sages worship you! You are Fire, the mouth to nectar at the time of sacrifices and offerings. Your strength is incomparable". Kadru's prayers did not go unanswered.

Dark clouds thundered. Heavy rains poured. Lightning flashed in the sky, producing magic. Sun's rays were blinded by Rain's arrows. The Nagas rejoiced and heaved a sigh of relief. Led by Vinata and Garuda, they soon arrived on the island in the ocean. It was a heavenly forest, full of trees, flowers and the breeze spreading the fragrances all around. It was full of sandalwood trees, a place for singing tribes, divine, peaceful and full of melodious birds. Kadru and her sons now wished to see another beautiful island and they ordered Garuda to take them. Garuda complained, to his mother.

Vinata explained that her sister had deceived her and that now she was her slave. She would have to do whatever, she was asked to do. The honourable son felt his mother's pain and anguish. Garuda started devising ways and means of taking his mother out of Kadru's web. Kadru and her sons demanded nectar in barter for his mother's freedom.

Vinata knew that her son was brave and strong. Before setting on the journey to get ambrosia, she advised him, "Garuda, you will encounter a number of obstacles and enemies. Do not be afraid. Fight them all and move on; whether it is the evil hunters living on the mountains or animals that come in your way. But never hurt or kill a humble learned soul. A wise scholar is supreme among all the classes. He is the father and the preceptor. He is the one who is invited to pray for the well being and happiness of our departed ancestors. If you provoke a noble man, he shall fight you back like no warrior does".

Vinata knew her son's strength and energy were unparalleled. She prayed to the Almighty Sun and the Moon to protect her son during the journey. She bid him farewell and engaged in prayers, for his peace, welfare, and successful accomplishment of the mission.

Garuda descended on the evil like Satan himself, eliminating them single handedly. The mountains close to the ocean too shook with the violence. In the process, he encountered a nautch woman with her noble husband. Garuda did not want to kill a teacher even if he was associated with those who were evil. He let both go, lest his anger destroy him. The Brahmin blessed him.

He successfully fought many people, who obstructed his way. Garuda now went to his father, Kashyapa, to seek his blessings. Kashyapa, advised him to continue fighting warring factions, be it animals or demons, so that he was strong enough to fight for nectar in the hands of good. Garuda, now, decided to fight, warring animals that obstructed his path.

The enmity between the tortoise and the elephant is known. Both these animals are like the great Vibhavasu and his younger brother Supratika. Supratika wanted his share in the family inheritance. He was not willing to maintain it jointly with his elder brother. Vibhavasu advised him against doing so. "Once the wealth is divided, love is replaced by enmity and selfishness in the guise of friendship. Others take advantage and add fuel to fire increasing the crisis. This leads to disaster and downfall of the warring brothers" he advised.

Supratika refused to see reason. Both the brothers wished ill of the other. Their relationship was more or less like the elephant and tortoise; both of low birth. Tortoise and the elephant both live in a large lake. Each is boastful of its strength and size. The moment one hears the other approach; he gets into the fight mode and wishes to kill the other.

Garuda eliminated the warring communities with ease was victorious and moved on. Garuda then went on an expedition to the city of Alamba. The place was heavenly. There were beautiful green trees adorned with fruits, looking like precious stone lapis lazuli. Everyone around the place trembled with fear on seeing Garuda the strong, powerful and radiant. All of them wanted the great Garuda to be their guest.

But the powerful one chose to live among the ascetics in their residence made of sandalwood. Now with so many people living, the dwelling collapsed. With no shelter, Garuda along with the fellow travelers and the tortoise and elephants among men, marched to Mount Gandhamadana, the best of indestructible mountains. Garuda's form was full of energy, strength and a mind as swift as wind, incapable of defeat.

Garuda, continued his journey, to the high mountains, covered with snowy peaks and inaccessible even in dreams. He was again accompanied by the demons, who were there with him right from the beginning of the journey. Now the path was too rocky and their resolve too weak. They ended up fighting, killing each other on the way. Those who did manage to reach the top, died, owing to the harshness shown by Rain. Garuda finally reached the snow covered peaks alone, shining like gold with the sun's brilliant rays. There the trees were adorned with flowers that shone like lightning in the sky.

But Garuda's journey was yet not over. The hurdles persisted. Rain hurled it's arrows on him persistently. The meteors and loosened rocks from the mountains, under Indra's persistent onslaught, attacked him from all angles. The mist, clouds and fog arose like smoke, darkening the beautiful landscape

Even nature did not want Garuda to succeed. It did not want ambrosia herbs to land in the hands of Nagas, for most of them had become vile and fearfully poisonous. But the strength and unparalleled energy of Garuda was amazing. He was giving a tough fight to Rain.

There were incessant blows by Rain, the Sun, Wind and all the natural forces of the universe. Garud fought them all valiantly. He roared in spite of the onslaught, from all sides. He did not tremble, showed no signs of tiring. He fought the attacking birds. But their beaks, talons and wings were not strong enough for his valour and strength.

Rain had retreated but the Sun and Wind did not give up. They created a barrier of flames and dust around nectar herbs. Garuda just walked through the inferno and reached very close to the herbs that would give his mother freedom from bondage. The last hurdle was the thorny bushes with sharp blades, which would eliminate the intruder in no time, swaying from end to end with the fierce Wind. Those bushes were home to fierce snakes, with venomous eyes and fiery tongues, as though they were jealously guarding the ambrosia herbs. Their fierceness did not deter the warrior. He hurled dust making them temporarily blind, and tore them to shreds. Like lightning he uprooted the herbs from the ground, and started his journey back home.

Sun's brilliance appeared to pale before Garuda's brilliant aura. The holy sky was amazed at the spectre. Garuda had resisted the temptation of consuming the herbs that would free him from disease and decay of the body. The sky blessed the valorous one with long life without disease and decay, and a strong body to travel from one place to another, swiftly, standing tall.

Rain was yet not satisfied. It struck his arrows. Garuda merely smiled back, and proudly announced that his spirit was indomitable. Rain in awe compared Garuda to Suparna, the bird with beautiful feathers. It extended his hand for friendship. Garuda felt humbled. He thought to himself, "One should never indulge in self praise, be it one's abilities or strength".

He was confident that without fatigue he could travel the mountains, forests and oceans that came his way. He prayed to the Almighty for forgiveness for taking away herbs that gave nectar. But he promised that they would never fall in the hands of the evil, lest they overcame and overpowered the noble ones.

He had a strong conviction that he was strong and powerful and could do whatever he wanted, but humbly bowed his head to the Almighty. He prayed to Him to help him eliminate the evil Nagas, who had enslaved his mother. With the herbs he proceeded to meet his mother.

Garuda handed them over to the Nagas and in turn freed his mother from their slavery.

The Nagas were overjoyed and elated. All of them went for a bath and purifying ritual before feasting on the magic herb of good health and longevity. In the meantime Rain started a heavy downpour and Wind created a hurricane. The herbs just vanished into thin air. On seeing the spectacle the Nagas felt deceived. In desperation they started licking the ground that had borne the herbs a little while ago.

Henceforth, Garuda lived peacefully with his mother Vinata, eliminating the wild Nagas that came his way. Vinata was delivered from the sin she had committed towards her son Aruna. She had been envious of her sister Kadru's sons and had neglected her own child at the time of birth that hence died. Kadru had mothered lots of strong and powerful Nagas. All of them were not vile and poisonous. But quite a few of them were, and had to be eliminated.

KADRU'S BROOD

Airavata, Takshaka and Shesha were among the prominent ones who were invincible and valorous. To do penance for his mother' Kadru's misdeeds Shesha left her and went to mount Gandhamadana and slopes of Himalayas. He undertook hazardous expeditions to atone for the sins his mother had committed and he was unwittingly part of it. His skin, muscles and flesh shrunk and hair got matted. But he was firm and resolute in his decision. "My brothers are wicked. They are jealous of each other. They showed no mercy towards Vinata, but instead helped mother Kadru in deceiving her. In spite of all their conniving, Garuda is much stronger than them. This is their punishment and reward. He has the blessings of our father Kashyapa, in his good deeds. I do not wish to have any association with my evil brothers, and shall engage in penance till I am no more", he thought to himself.

Shesha prayed that he be delivered from the bonds of his evil family and lead him to the path of peace and tranquillity. It appears as though the burden of the entire earth with its good, evil and uncertainties is on Shesha's large, wise and peaceful head.

Vinata's son Garuda became powerful Shesha's companion. The good stood united. Kadru and her vile sons out of arrogance had incurred the wrath of lots of wise people, who had come in their contact. In fun and frolic, out of apathy, they had harmed many and did not even repent. Parikshit, father of Janemajaya, had been killed by one such Naga. Janemajaya was inconsolable when he learnt of the truth. He vowed to eliminate them all.

BIRTH OF ASTIKA

The Nagas now feared for their life. They all got in a huddle. They started finding ways and means, to condone for the wrong done by them and dousing fire of Janemajaya's anger; in barter for their life. Vasuki, the king of the Nagas and Airavrata were the wise among the lot. The brothers started suggesting ways and means, to avert the calamity and save their lives.

Some were of the opinion that it would be best to disguise as ascetics and beg him to stop. Some thought, the wise among them should become the king's advisors and advise him against such an act, reflecting on the serious evils of it. Or else, one possibility would be to kill the chief of the army, who would be anointed to perform the sacrifice. But everyone was wary of killing an innocent one.

But suggestions kept pouring in. Some even suggested invoking Rain, to bring a downpour on the sacrificial fire and dousing it while others suggested killing everyone participating in the sacrifice. Well the vilest of all was, killing the root of all afflictions, the king himself.

But when confronted with danger, the remedy should be based on Justice and not on unlawful tactics, lest it destroys the entire universe. To die in the Naga sacrifice, to be conducted by Janemajaya, was a result of destiny and remedy lay in destiny alone.

Kadru wished her sons dead for not being of use to her in her malicious intents. In spite of the harshness of a mother's heart, the universe endorsed her. Her sons the Nagas had multiplied innumerably and most of them were poisonous, mean, full of valour but cruel and would attack for no reason. But there were some who followed goodness. They had to be saved from the terrible danger when time came. The wicked ones would meet their fate.

Elaptara, the wise among them suggested, giving their sister Jaratkaru in marriage to a noble soul. Their offspring would be like the father who would bring an end to the sacrifice and the virtuous Nagas would be able to escape. This would be in tune with laws of righteousness. Everyone applauded at the noble suggestion.

In the meantime Vasuki kept suffering. His fear for the life of his innocent brothers but not the evil ones made him restless. He engaged his brothers in keeping an eye on the noble sage Jaratkaru, in an effort to offer his sister's hand, whenever he desired to get married. The Nagas trusted Vasuki. He was the king and a humble benefactor.

On the other hand, Jaratkaru practiced austerities, engaged in deep knowledge, learning without fear. However he showed no desire for a wife or offspring.

DEATH OF PARIKSHIT

During that period, there was the great Kuru king Parikshit. Like his grandfather Arjun, he was a supreme archer. One day while on a hunting trip he shot a deer with an arrow. In the past no animal had managed to escape death at Parikshit's hands but this one got lost in the thick forest. Parikshit went in its pursuit but came very close to death himself.

He came across a hermit under rigid vows of silence. The hermit did not answer any queries regarding the deer or when asked for water to quench his thirst. Out of anger he placed a dead snake around the hermit's shoulders. The hermit still did not react but continued looking on. The king's anger ebbed and he relented. Eventually he returned to his kingdom in Hastinapur.

The hermit had an equally intelligent learned son Shringi. He was intelligent as his father but prone to quick bouts of anger. One day his friend Krishna, a Brahmin himself, light heartedly commented, "No matter, how learned Brahmin community is, practises austerities, but still has to be subservient to the mighty kings! The carcass of a snake around your father's shoulder is a symbol of dominance of the king over the full of prowess and learned ascetics".

Shringi's anger, arrogance and pride on hearing this, poisoned him. "What wrong had my father done to the evil king? He shall pay for his evil deeds and I will make sure he does." Shringi found the king's action abominable. He felt that the king was vile, evil hearted, had no respect for the learned ascetics and was a disgrace to the illustrious Kuru lineage. He talked about it to his friend, Takshaka, the lord of the Nagas.

Takshaka swift, virulent and poisonous, taken in by Shringi's emotional outburst, agreed to eliminate the king. Shringi still enraged, went back home and told his father of his resolve to decimate the Kuru heir.

Shamika, Shringi's father reprimanded, "Son, teachers get the patronage of the kings and are protected by them. Had it not been for the king who follows the path of goodness himself, we would suffer many afflictions and not merits. We should be magnanimous enough to forget the evil act. The king was not aware of my vow of silence. He himself is a humble man and does not deserve to die."

Shringi, steadfast in his views continued to explain, "Father, I have already made up my mind and gone ahead to execute my plan. This is not a trivial issue. The king will have to pay for this misdemeanour."

Shamika continued to try hard, to make his son see sense. "Son, I don't doubt your immense wisdom. You have lots of integrity and truthfulness in you. But there is lots of anger too. Anger, takes us away from the path of goodness. It takes away all merits one obtains through gruelling hard work and knowledge. Righteousness and tranquillity leads to success in life. Forgiveness brings peace. With tranquillity and forgiveness, it is not difficult to conquer anger. Once we are in control of our senses, no one can defeat us".

The ascetic immediately sent, his disciple, Gouramukha, to the king, asking forgiveness for his son's brash act of immaturity and ignorance. He warned the king of the imminent attack on him, by the Naga king Takshaka. He sharply admonished his son, asking him to weigh his father's words carefully, tone down his temperament and never assume himself too grown up to ignore the wisdom bestowed on him by his father. A father's advice always leads the child onto the path of success.

Gouramukha announced the purpose of his visit to Parikshit. The king at once recalled the unfortunate incident that had occurred in the forest when he had gone hunting. He felt ashamed of his evil doing and was crestfallen on learning that the hermit was under vow of silence at that point of time. He abhorred himself when told that that Shamika had forgiven him out of compassion.

A humble man himself Parikshit grieved over the heinous crime he had committed. He in all humility begged Shamika for forgiveness and conveyed it to the messenger.

Death frightens one and sundry, no matter how brave. Parikshit got the doors of his palace locked, heavily guarded and had all the royal physicians in attendance, whenever the need arose. Satisfied that he had fortified himself against death, he continued to carry on his royal duties. But death is destiny, which no one can escape.

Both Takshaka and Kashyapa crossed paths. One was going to take the king to the heavenly abode and other to obstruct the way of Satan. Both exhibited their strength. Takshaka uprooted a massive tree, with just one blow. Kashyapa with his intelligence and learning brought it back to life. He took a sapling from the tree and planted it, which would eventually become a tree in no time.

But Kashyapa was no ordinary mortal. He had vision. He possessed unsurpassable wisdom. He knew a person's lifespan was predetermined. No doctor had the power to alter it. So there was no point going against laws of nature. It would be an exercise in futility. It would only bring disgrace to his illustrious name.

Moreover Parikshit in anger had unintentionally committed a grave sin. He had hurt and demeaned a good noble soul without provocation. He would have to absolve himself of the crime. This would be retribution. Kashyapa departed and went back home.

Takshaka along with other Nagas dressed as ascetics continued their onward journey to meet the king. They performed religious rites and offered fruits and water to the king. The holy offerings were distributed among everyone in the court.

Parikshit saw a very small poisonous worm in his fruit. He was at peace with himself. He wished to honour Shringi's words, an ascetic. Evil act should not go unpunished so that goodness shall prevail. Smiling at himself he ate the fruit. He died peacefully. Takshaka was the messenger, spreading good and eliminating evil. The royal advisors, Brahmins and priests performed the funeral rites. The subjects and the advisors placed Parikshit's young son on the throne. They named him Janamejaya meaning the slayer of enemies.

Janamejaya though very young was wise and brave. He ruled the kingdom like his great grandfather Yudhishthira. Janamejaya married Vapushtama, the daughter of king Suvarnavarnam. Vapushtama was beautiful like the fairy Urvashi who had married the Kuru King Pururava. Both husband and wife enjoyed intense love and marital bliss.

JARATKARU AND HIS TIMES

Jaratkaru, the learned sage, engaged in austerities and acquiring vast storehouse of knowledge, travelled all around the earth, visiting holy places and living fruitfully. One day while sleeping he witnessed a strange vision. His ancestors had gone very old; they were mere rags and bones. Time never stops for anyone. It quickly passes by. There were no youngsters around. He saw his own shadow amongst them. But that too was, of a man entering old age.

The vast knowledge, the ancestors treasured was fading, growing dim.

There was no one to whom they could pass it on. He was their only offspring and he too would be in their shoes, in no time. Jaratkaru in his dream walked up to them, and offered help. They refused, for he was celibate, had not married, and had no young one. In spite of his learning and noble living he was of no use to them.

Jaratkaru, got up from his slumber with a start, sweating and perplexed. He was getting old and needed children, to whom he could pass on his immense knowledge. With great knowledge and high thoughts, it is equally important, we have children to whom we can pass on the legacy lest all goes waste and that would be a sin.

Jaratkaru was agitated and could no longer concentrate on his daily chores. One day while walking absentmindedly in the forest, he came across the Naga king Vasuki. He narrated his ordeal. He wanted a wife who was learned, noble like him, had a mind of her own and would not be dependent on him for her upkeep and well being. She should be willing to marry him, on her own accord without force, at her own free will. Her name should literally mean Jaratkaru. Vasuki offered his sister's hand, who was a great ascetic herself, for marriage, to the great sage. He accepted all his conditions unanimously.

Vasuki had been waiting for this day for very long. With lots of humility, without any expectations and full honour, he wished to give her away. Jaratkaru, thus married Vasuki's sister, with full religious rites and ceremonies, and moved in with her to the house built by her brother. He categorically made it clear that he would leave her the moment he felt humiliated or insulted by her behaviour.

Vasuki's sister served him with lots of love, humility, watchfulness of a dog and alertness of a crow. Both of them set up home and hearth with love. One day she reminded her husband to continue with his learning lest life of domesticity, interfere with his higher pursuits of life. Jaratkaru took offence at being reminded of his duties.

He felt he was someone with great knowledge and bearing and no one had to teach him his duties. In anger he left the grieving maiden, even though she was only assisting him in his purpose of life. But fate was not that cruel. Her husband had left her for no fault of hers, but had been already impregnated by her man. She took solace in the knowledge that her brother Vasuki had given her in marriage to save their lineage from annihilation and that purpose had been fulfilled. The son born from her union with Jaratkaru would act as a saviour for all the wise and noble Nagas.

Vasuki and the Naga clan looked after the sister, with lots of reverence and kindness. The embryo in her womb grew radiant like the blazing sun and the heavenly moon. At the appropriate time the child came into being. He was the heir to Jaratkaru's illuminous lineage and saviour of his mother's Naga clan.

Vasuki's sister as brilliant as Jaratkaru himself raised him. Sage Chyavana, son of Brighu tutored him in literature and philosophy. The boy was named Astika. His father had said "asti", meaning he is there in the womb to his mother, before leaving her to move back to his life in the forest. Even as a child Astika was brilliant, disciplined well looked after by all the Nagas.

On the other hand, king Janamejaya was extremely perplexed about the mystery surrounding his father's death. He wished to know everything good and evil associated with his father. His most wise minister gave him a fair account. Parikshit was a wise man. He treated his subjects impartially without hate or love but with utmost honesty.

A great warrior himself the science of war and weaponry, adorned him. All classes, teachers, warriors, craftsmen and the lower rung in the hierarchy were treated equally. Even the widows, orphans, disabled and the poor gathered under his protective umbrella. When the Kuru lineage was taking its last breath, he was born in Uttara's womb as Arjun''s grandson, and thus came to be known as Parikshit.

Wise advisors guided him. All the six vices- anger, desire, greed, ego, delusion and envy never touched him. He was always in complete control of his senses. His rule lasted for almost sixty years. His death was predestined to be undertaken by the Nagas. On learning that his father, was just like his illustrious grandfather Arjun, benevolent, just and kind towards his subjects, he was even more intrigued." How could such a noble man meet a violent end, like the one Parikshit had?" he wondered.

The wise minister then told him, of the hunting expedition episode. He recounted how Parikshit, a great archer, spent most of his time hunting, leaving the administration of the State in the hands of efficient ministers. During one of his hunting sprees, he came across Shamika, in the forest, who was at that time, under vow of silence. Shamika did not answer any of Parikshit's queries. The king was thirsty, hungry and had no clue that the sage was observing a vow of silence. In anger he abused him violently.

The wise one did not retaliate for he knew that the act was carried out unintentionally. But his son Shringi could not control his anger. He wished revenge on the man who had humiliated his father, a man free of pettiness, avarice and jealousy, pure in word and practice. Without consulting even Shamika, his father, he asked his Naga friend Takshaka, to kill the king.

When Shamika learnt of his son's immaturity and indiscretion, he immediately got the king warned, of the impending danger to his life.

The wise minister told Janamejaya, about Kashyapa's and Takshaka's meeting in the jungle. He told him of the witness to the episode, a man, who had climbed the tree to collect firewood.

How the tree was uprooted by the mighty Takshaka and how Kashyapa planted a sapling, to revive the tree and with his immense knowledge and learning, cured the man who fell almost dead from the uprooted tree. The man then went to the city and told everyone around of what he saw and heard.

Janemajaya's heart wrenched in pain and agony. On Shringi's insistence, Takshaka had killed his father. The king too wanted Shringi's curse to not go unabated, for a Brahmin's pronouncement should never be negated at any cost. But, he felt Takshaka should not have at the same time with his devious, glib words and logic prevented Kashyapa from performing his duty of curing his father when attacked.

Kashyapa was a holy ascetic. His quest for glory and fame prevented him from doing his duty. On the other hand Takshaka's evil mindedness killed the invincible king. Takshaka committed a grave sin by preventing a Brahmin from performing his duty. Janamejaya wanted, Takshaka to pay for his sins and his father avenged. Hence the king and his ministers vowed to eliminate all the Nagas in the forest.

Janamejaya along with the royal priests, held a prayer session, invoking the blessing of god and his ancestors. He prayed to the Almighty to give him strength and courage to punish Takshaka and his relations, for their evil deeds without provocation. He wished to set on fire the forest where they lived, and bring a conclusive end to his duty.

There was a bard among the priests, who was extremely intelligent. He felt there were discrepancies in the king's decision. All the Nagas were not evil, so it would be unfair to kill all. He hoped Nature would never let such an unjust act to materialise. The great forest in which all the Nagas lived was set on fire.

The Nagas old, young and children slowly starting perishing in the fire that had started. There were many Brahmins who prayed for the success of Janamejaya's mission. They recited verses from rig veda, sam veda, yajur veda and from atharva veda. All these Brahmins were the officiating priests at the prayer meeting organised by the king for the success of his mission. The Nagas started getting burnt in the forest fire taking their last breath. Takshaka the King ran, away from the forest and took refuge in the rain forest. He confessed his evil deed and made home his forest, that had rains throughout the year.

But Vasuki continued to be there with the heat emanating from the burning fire, making him weak. He was losing consciousness of his being, wandering and waiting for fire to engulf him. He felt absolutely helpless. He knew the forest fire would not be stopped until and unless, the entire forest was burnt down and their race obliterated. Janamejaya would stop nothing short of that.

Vasuki in desperation went up to his sister and requested her to send her son Astika, who was a learned Brahmin and whom everybody respected to Janamejaya. The king himself was a wise man and would understand what the other learned one was saying. It was an attempt to stop the killing of innocent Nagas along with the evil ones. The innocent ones needed to be saved from extermination.

Vasuki's sister also named Jaratkaru, like her illustrious husband, both in deed and word, called upon her son Astika. She explained to him as to why she was married off to the aging sage Jaratkaru by her brother Vasuki. She also told him as to how Kadru considered to be mother of all Nagas out of anger and deviousness wished all her sons dead at the hands of a mighty king. But the Universe too wished the same. Surprisingly his reasons were different. It felt that the Nagas had multiplied many forth and most of them were very lethal without provocation. Vasuki, Kadru's son tried out ways and means to stop injustice.

When the ocean was churned by Brahma, he went there and after lots of penance got nectar which he never used himself or gave to any of his brothers, an elixir which would make the Nagas invincible. He very humbly offered it to his departed ancestors and prayed for solace. After lots of soul searching, he felt, he should give his brilliant sister Jaratkaru, to a wise scholar. Their progeny too would be learned and wise. Only an intelligent person would make the king listen and see reason and save nagas from annihilation. Further she requested Astika to fulfil his purpose of life for which he was born, and for which she was given in marriage to the sage Jaratkaru.

Wise that he was, he fully absorbed the gravity of the situation. He assured his uncle Vasuki and mother of his help, and asked them to free their mind of any fear that may befall the nagas. Even though he was a young he was always honest, truthful and full of wise thoughts. He wished to befriend the king and win his trust with his learning. Later, he wanted to advise the king, against the futility of such an act, which involved the killing of innocent nagas too, along with the evil.

Having amply reassured Vasuki, he went ahead with his mission. Soon he was on his way to meet Janamejaya. To gain access to the king, he showed massive appreciation for the prayer meet comparing it to the ones performed by Krishna Dwaipayna. He went on to praise the king for all the good qualities he possessed. He compared Janemjaya to Yama for his perseverance, to Sun in splendour, to Bhishama in rigidity of vows, to Valmiki in firmness and to Vashishtha in controlling anger.

The king and the Brahmins present at the prayer meeting were pleased with his wise words. Janamejaya wished to grant a boon to the scholar who was but a child. Astika had earned the respect of the king with his learning and wisdom. On the other hand the Brahmins present at the prayer meeting wished the king would first concentrate on completing his mission of Naga sacrifice, lest some hurdle came in the way.

Lohitaksha and the Brahmins present knew that Takshaka had moved to another forest out of fear blessed by Indra. He had all the patronage of Indra and Fire would not touch him. They expressed their concern but the king would not hear of anything. The priests carried on with their prayers and made holy offerings to Fire.

Indra arrived with Takshaka in tow, in the forest, which Janemjaya had set on fire. But the king's honest desire to punish the wrongdoer and Brahma's justice weighed heavily on the otherwise invincible Indra. Fire countered Indra with all its might. Indra left Takshaka to his own devices and bid adieu. The Naga king's cries could be heard in the entire forest. The Brahmins performing the prayers heaved a sigh of relief for their mission had almost reached a conclusive end.

They told Janamejaya, that the time was ripe to grant the Brahmin child a boon. The king agreed. Astika wished that the king would stop the mindless killing of Nagas and protect his mother's lineage. Janemjaya was aghast. He did not want to incur the wrath of a Brahmin, but at the same time could not grant what he wanted. He had waited patiently for so long for this moment to arrive. Takshaka, his noble father's decimator was about to meet his end.

He implored the Brahmin to ask for any other boon but this. The child was adamant. The Brahmins present at the prayer meeting advised Janmejaya, to grant Astika his wish. In accordance with Brahma's wishes, lots of Nagas lost their lives, in the sacrificial fire of the forest. Some were from Vasuki's lineage, some from Takshaka's and many from Airavata's. There were also Nagas from Kouravya and Dhrithrashtra's lineage.

All of them were extremely swift, poisonous and powerful who would attack without provocation. Sons, grandsons, progenies fell in the fire. Some had gigantic bodies and could travel from one place to another in no time. They were all burnt.

In accordance to Astika's wish, Janemjaya ordered the fire in the forest to be stopped. Takshaka just got saved by the fraction of a second. Parikshit son's sacrifice came to an end. When Astika was granted his boon the thundering clouds clapped in joy. The king was happy. He distributed gifts and riches among the Brahmins and men present.

Lohitaksha's doubts at the beginning of the prayer meet were pacified. The fire sacrifice concluded on a positive note. The king with great respect invited Astika to the horse sacrifice. Astika's mother and uncle were delighted. Astika wanted people to learn from his virtuous deeds and actions with a peaceful mind and free themselves of any fear that haunts them. Astika left behind many sons and grandsons to carry on the Brighu lineage.

CHAPTER SIX
Adi-vamshavatarana

Krishna Dvaipayana was born to Satyavati and sage Parashara. He mastered many texts and had illustrious progenies Pandu, Dhritarashtra and Vidhur to continue Shantanu's lineage. He was a great poet. Having learnt that his great grandson Janamejaya was holding a prayer service in the presence of a large gathering of wise men and kings, he went accompanied by his disciple Vaishampayana and many other learned ones. Janemajaya welcomed him with lots of honour and love.

As per rituals he washed his grandfather's feet and hands and in all humbleness offered oblations. The feelings were reciprocated wholeheartedly. Both the luminaries exchanged notes of well being. Janamejaya requested his great grandfather to narrate stories of his illustrious ancestors, the Kurus, as he was the sole witness.

Janamejaya's mind always raked with unsaid questions. He wondered, as to why his ancestors great and virtuous quarrelled at all. And still more, why did the great battle take place, which eventually decimated almost the entire Kuru lineage. Dvaiyapayna instructed his disciple Vaishampayana to recite the entire journey of the Kauravs and the Pandavs. Vaishampayna narrated in totality without bias, the basis of the fight between the Kauravs and the Pandavs and the destruction it brought.

Vaishampayana narrated the events exactly as he had heard from Krishna Dwaipayana absolute in accomplishments to the assembly of great scholars, kings and best of all to the heir, Janamejaya. Thus he went.

After the death of their father Pandu, the Pandavas returned home, to their kingdom Hastinapur, from the forest. They acquired mastery in art of warfare and archery. The Kauravas envied the Pandavas for their physical strength, energy and skill. The five brothers had the respect of the people of Hastinapur.

Envy and evil mindedness drove Duryodhana, the eldest Kaurava mad. With the help of his friend Karna and Shakuni, he devised means and ways of humiliating and hurting the Pandavs. But Vidhur was always on his heels counter foiling the oppressive evil doers. Vidhur was guardian angel to the orphaned Pandavs ensuring their safety and happiness.

Destiny protected the five brothers with its embalming touch. On the other hand Duryodhan's anger and envy prevented him from taking any rational decision. With the help of his friend Karna, brother Duhshasana and others, and not to forget his father Dhritrashtra's consent, he decided to char the Pandavs to death in sleep and eliminate any competition and heartbreak consequently. But fate had anointed Vidhur as the Pandav's caretaker. He got the brothers and their mother evacuated to a safe place through an underground tunnel built from the house before Duryodhan could set the house on fire.

In the forest Bhim overpowered and killed the evil Hidimba who oppressed the poor villagers. Later the brothers along with their mother moved to the town of Ekachakra. Then onwards they lived in disguise as ascetics lest become victims of Duryodhan's connivance again. Later Draupadi joined the family.

Once recognised all of them moved back to Hastinapur. Dhritrashtra advised them to forget their enmity and start a new life in Khandvaprastha which had many new towns and roads. They were given wealth from the royal treasury. Kunti and her sons established themselves in their new abode.

Fine warriors that they were, accomplished in the art of warfare, they brought many neighbouring kingdoms under their control. The ones who refused to accept their sovereignty were defeated. But power was attained with honesty and calm. Kingdoms in all the four directions were under their control. It appeared as though six suns shone in the universe.

Later, as per the designated rules Arjun was in exile in a forest for a period of twelve years and a month. During that period he married Vasudev's younger sister Subhadra. Subhadra considered it her good fate to be married to a Pandav brother. With with the help of Vasudev, the Pandavas burnt down the Khandava forest. With the help of the chariot, that almost appeared to fly and Gandhiva a weapon with infinite number of arrows, both Arjun and Krishna managed to free Maya, the demon who lived in Khandvaprastha.

Maya paid back the debt by building a celestial assembly hall full of beautiful and precious stones. Unfortunately Maya's good intentions invoked avarice in Duryodhan. With deceit, in connivance with his uncle Shakuni, he defeated them, packing them again off to the forest for a period of thirteen years. On their return from exile, Duryodhan refused to part with their kingdom Khandvaprastha. Thus followed the great battle eliminating almost the entire kshatriya lineage with an exception of few.

Certain issues are full of intrigue. One wonders as to why in the battle of Kurukshetra Pandavas lost men who did not deserve to die but still are worshipped! Bhim had intense strength and energy but he allowed himself to be oppressed! Yudhishthira lost his entire kingdom in a wager he had with Duryodhana. However his brothers continued to follow him! Yudhisthira, follower of virtuous path and son of Dharma suffered a lot. Arjun a great warrior who could send any warrior to the lap of death underwent lots of oppression! Krishna Dvaipayna composed this work for the welfare of the generations to come and spreading fame of the Pandavas and high energy warriors.

BIRTH OF SATYAVATI

During that period, there was king Uparichara of the Puru lineage. He ruled over Chedi with devotion and righteousness. Upset over the futility of weapons and wars the king renounced his kingdom and subjects, and started living in a hermitage practising austerities. But the king's mind was always in turmoil.

There was a constant debate going on as to whether he had done justice to himself and his subjects. One day the king was fast asleep. It rained hard. Apparently Indra was answering Uparichara's unsaid questions.

Path of righteousness does not come with austerities alone. It comes with merit and virtue obtained by hard labour. Oh king, live among your people and kingdom that is full of prosperity and has blessings of Brahma. Your subjects are content, pious and free from all falsehood engaged in their duties. They shall make you proud. I shall give you a chariot that runs very fast and appears as though it were flying. You just need a bamboo staff to protect yourself and your people. I shall bless you with the virtue of invincibility that shall always protect you in war.

The king got up from his sleep as though in a trance. He went back to his kingdom and got bamboo trees planted everywhere. The entire kingdom along with the king, worshipped the bamboo trees with garlands and ornaments. Apparently Indra was smiling and bestowing good fortune and blessings over the people of Chedi. Vasu ruled Chedi with righteousness and protected the earth.

Uparichara's five sons surpassed even him in valour and strength. They were invincible. They established separate dynasties and named cities and towns after themselves. Vasu himself continued to travel throughout the kingdom, worshipped by all. People called him Uparichara meaning someone from a higher plane.

The great river Shuktimati flowed through the kingdom. The river changed course and started flowing through the crevices of the great mountain Kolahola. Due to tectonic movement of the earth's plates the sand gave way and a river started flowing through the mountain. A whole colony of settlements grew around the river.

Orphaned twins, a brother and sister who considered the river as their home lived there. Uparichara married the girl Girihika and made her brother the chief of the army. Girihika was as beautiful and virtuous as goddess herself. Vasu wished to enlarge his brood through the lady when she was at the right time of her period, lest it would go barren. But as fate would have it, the king had to go on an important task relating to his kingdom. His entourage camped on the banks of river Yamuna.

He saw a beautiful nymph Adrika, from the fishermen community; it reminded him of his wife Girihika. The king had twins from her. Uparichara, accepted the son Matysa but gave away the daughter back to the fishermen community. Adrika, in turn, gave up her human body, having fulfilled her task of being a mother.

Her daughter Satyavati grew up among the fishermen. Satyavati like her mother was very beautiful. She had immense character and qualities. She plied a boat across the Yamuna. One day, the great ascetic Parashar saw her when he was on a pilgrimage. He was bewitched by her beauty. Even the damsel was taken in by his youth and character. Both of them wished to unite. The rishi did not care for his vows and the damsel for her virginity. Their love was pure and not unholy or dark.

BIRTH OF VEDVYASA

Soon Satyavati gave birth to a son Ved Vyasa of immense learning. She was no longer the low, boat plying, fish smelling woman but a charming young lady who had the love and child of an ascetic of holy deeds. Later Parashar went ahead on his destined path practising austerities and learning. He did not let domesticity stop him.

When old enough the son Krishna Dvaipayna too took leave from his mother Satyavati to follow his father's footsteps. But the boy true to his character promised to come whenever she needed him. People started regarding her Gandhavati, a virtuous woman.

Krishna Dvaipayna was born to Satyavati and the great scholar Parashara, on the island of Yamuna. He knew thoroughly well that with the passage of time and with the passing of every era– satya, treta, dvapara and kali, people would lose out on virtues and character. As a tribute to Universe and Justice, Dvaipayna classified the verses of Mahabharat for posterity. He taught Mahabharata to his son Shuka, disciple Vaishampayna and to Sumantu, Paila and Jaimini.

Bhishma, successor of Shantanu, was the son of Ganga, after whom the great river is named. Justice and righteousness is not only restricted to an individual and his way of livelihood. Animandavya a young, educated man though suspected to be a thief, was not a thief.

Vidhur upholder of just beliefs, learned, righteous and pure was born to a royal housekeeper, considered to be from the lower strata of society. In the same way, Sanjaya, Dhritrashtra's charioteer, gifted with divine intellect and sagaciousness was born to Gavalgana, a charioteer. Karna was born to Kunti when she was still a virgin. He was reared and brought up by a charioteer. But he had all the qualities of an inborn warrior and was said to be wearing a natural armour and earrings at the time of birth.

Vasudev having all the qualities of a warrior and scholar was born from Devaki in the Andhakas and Vrishnis lineage, spreading righteousness in the universe. Sage Bharadvaja was the father of Dronacharya, who taught Kshatriya princes the art of warfare. Sage Goutama gave birth to Kripa and Kripi. Kripi was Ashvathama's mother and Drona was his father. The great warrior Dhrishtadyumna said to be born with a bow in his hand destroyed Drona.

Draupadi was beautiful and had lots of inner strength. Prahlada's disciples were Nagnajit and Subala. Shakuni and Gandhari were Subala's children, skilled in material pursuits, damned by bad intentions. Vichitravirya's children Dhritrashtra, Pandu and Vidhur were born of Krishna Dvaipayna. Pandu's five children were born of ascetics of unsurpassable strength. Most of them have qualities of righteousness, honesty and vast knowledge.

Dhritrashatra had lots of children and one son Yuyutsu from an intercaste liaison. Yuyutsu had a vaishya mother. Abhimanyu the great warrior was Arjun's son born of Vasudev's sister Subhadra. Draupadi had five sons from the five Pandav brothers. It was Prativindhya from Yudhisthira, Sutasoma from Vrikoda, Shrutakirti from Arjuna, Shataruke from Nakula and Shrutasena from Sahdeva.

Bhima also had a son Ghatotchaka from Hidimbi in the forest. Draupada, king of Panchala had a daughter Shikandini. Shikandini's sexual orientation was different. Later in life she became Shikandi, a brave warrior.

During that period Parashar a sage, out of outrage and injustice suffered, eliminated the evil warriors till his friends collectively intervened and requested him to stop. It appeared as though the entire warrior race had come to an end. In role reversal, someone from the calm, composed ascetics lineage had taken on the powerful kshatriyas.

Parashar then went to mount Mahendra and continued living there. The world now bereft of powerful warriors had no one else but the learned men to fall on. Their women went to sages to beget children. Powerful kshatriya women gave birth to many powerful warriors.

Warrior race surprisingly originated from the peaceful, well informed and enlightened ascetics. The new generation followed righteous path and conduct. Society was classified into different stratas depending on the profession a person practised. Intellectuals and well read ones were placed at the top. Righteousness was the guiding principle. Earth was once again governed righteously by the warriors with the learned as the preceptor and head. Wrong doers were justly punished. Indra showered blessings on warriors in the form of abundant fruitful rain.

All the stratas followed their duties diligently. Kshatriyas fought wars, gave alms to the poor. Brahmans studied literature, philosophy and taught Kshatriya children the art of warfare. Vaishyas were mainly farmers and tradesmen. Shudras carried on with the low and servile jobs. Universe prospered and shone brightly with green trees, coloured flowers and fruits at the right time. This was the Treta yug.

CHAPTER SEVEN
Sambhava Parva

Demons and nagas were the ones whose ideologies were in conflict with the good. Most of them were known to be proud, vain, power seekers. But evil could not touch great men even in infancy. Great teachers and scholars were good among men.

Shukra was the son of an ascetic. But he was the preceptor of demons. Even his four sons were preceptors to Asuras. Garuda, Arunia and many more were Vinata's sons. Vasuki, Shesha, Takshaka were Kadru's famous sons. Prava gave birth to divine Gandharvas, the singing and dancing community.

King Daksha had only daughters but did not have a son. He made his daughters his putrikas, wherein daughter returns to father's house after marriage with husband or the father adopts the daughter's son as his own.

With the evolution of universe, came into existence animals that were at a transition stage, slowly becoming humans with large heads, known as kimpurush. Brihaspati's sister, unattached to the world but attached to yoga, married Prabhasa. From the union was born Vishvakarma, founder of all crafts, maker of ornaments and chariots. Vishvakarma is worshipped till date as the founder father of craftsmanship.

Kashyapa, was the father to both the good and the demons. In other words Kashyapa is the father of universe.

Richika had an illustrious son Jamadgani. Parashurama, Jamadgani's son was well versed in the art of warfare and has been touted as the destroyer of warriors.

When people started devouring each other's food, Injustice, was born. It gave birth to lots of demons. From them were born fear, dread and death.

Drona, son of Bharadvaja, had great energy and performed great deeds. He had great skills and knowledge of weapons. At the same time he was well versed in the study of Philosphy. He brought fame to his lineage. His son Ashvathamma, even more valorous, was feared by the enemies. But Ashvathamma himself was under the influence of desire and anger.

Shantanu gave birth to many sons from wife Ganga. Bhishma, the youngest was very intelligent, a threat to enemy armies and an umbrella for the Kurus. He is known to have fought Rama, Jamadagani's son. Kripa, embodiment of virility, had ascetic parentage. Shakuni, tormentor of enemies, as known to the world, was a great warrior and scholar. Kritavarma, was a bull among warriors. Virata, king of unparalleled deeds was born to unknown parents.

DUSHANTA AND SHAKUNTALA SAGA

The Pourava dynasty was initiated by Dushanta. His subjects were Mlecchas. They were devoted to justice and righteousness. He was a great warrior who was capable of fighting on horseback and on elephants alike. Sun's radiance adorned him. His subjects lived in perfect harmony with themselves and with nature. They had the blessings of Indra, Sun and Moon. Hence the earth was adorned with plentiful crop.

The king would often go to the forest for hunting. Powerful horses, elephants with their mounts, a strong army with clubs, maces, javelins and swords accompanied him. The elephants trumpeted, the horses neighed in awe. Women, men and children would come out of their houses and shower flowers on the valiant king, tiger among men. They would follow the king and his entourage of brave warriors.

Happy with the adulations and love of his people, he would proceed towards the forest, to hunt. Once, a short distance before entering the forest he requested his subjects to return, back home. The king himself flew on his chariot into the forest like Suparna, the king of birds. The forest was truly heavenly. It was adorned by bilva, arka, khadira and dhava trees. It extended far and wide, strewn with uneven mountains and valleys. It was full of deer and their families. Many deer got pierced with his arrows.

Many families of tigers that got in his way were decimated. The forest shook with the strength of the king and his warriors, who gave the animals a befitting standoff. Most of them fled. Tiredness, exhaustion, thirst and hunger, dampened everyone's spirits. Some warriors were eaten by the hungry tigers; others were trampled by the elephants gone mad by arrow attacks. The king rained arrows in protest settling the mayhem.

He killed the wild animals running amuck. Along with his warriors he left and went to the neighbouring forest to hunt deer. The forest was dense. The king did not wish to risk the life of his warriors. He ordered them to halt at the foot of the forest and set out to explore the wilderness all by himself.

The trees swarmed with bees, humming melodious songs. The wind and gentle breeze shook the trees and showered the path with flowers. The singing of birds in tandem produced a musical effect in the whole forest. Brahma, it appeared was showering blessings and smiling on his subjects. The bright varied colours of the flowers appeared to dress the forest in happiness. The beauty and holiness of the place was enhanced by the ascetics, that dwelled there.

The forest was situated on a delta formed by the river. River Malini flowed through the forest making the hermitages appear ethereal. The place was delightful in its character. Ascetics, predators and deer lived in harmony.

The king's chariot flew unabated. The melodious singing of the birds filled the place. Holy chants vibrated in the background. Kinnaras and monkeys jumped all over the place. Elephants, deer, wild geese roamed uninhibited. The scenario was a visual delight. The echoes of the dancing peacocks and the churning waters of Ganga, filled the place.

The king entered further deep into the woods. He wished to meet Kanva. He instructed his cavalry, charioteers and infantry to wait at the footsteps of the hermit's abode. He entered the hermitage with only his priest and advisor like any other ordinary man of his kingdom.

Vedas and Samhitas were being recited in full metre and tone. The ascetics present were well versed in the principle of logic and self realization. Some were trained in rituals, some in rites for salvation, others in arguments for establishing truth and weeding out falsehood with philosophy.

The king felt as though he was in heaven on earth. The king went ahead, without his priest and advisor in search of Kanva. He called out aloud for him on not seeing him on his designated seat.

A pretty maiden appeared and announced that her father had gone out to collect fruits. She was attired in simple clothes. She introduced herself as Kanva's daughter Shakuntala. The king was intrigued. Kanva was an ascetic, who followed rigid austerities and had never known to father a child. Shakuntala sensed his dilemma. She narrated as to what she had overheard her father say to someone when he was asked the same question.

BIRTH OF SHAKUNTALA

Shakuntala's biological father was the great warrior sage Vishvamitra. His radiance even outshone Sun's. Menaka a heavenly beauty, out of whim and willfulness took upon herself the task of distracting the rishi from his path of austerities and learning. She knew that the task would be challenging. In spite of the energy and wisdom, Vishvamitra was prone to quick bouts of anger. He was born in a family of warriors but had become a recluse and spent his time learning. It would not be easy to seduce a man with so much internal strength and whose senses were in complete control, Maneka had wandered. She further mulled over his towering stature. His eyes reflected wisdom and righteous anger. His tongue whipped honesty.

Everyone who knew him was in awe of his towering personality. Menaka's heart filled with love and desire. She meekly entered the hermitage and paid homage. The ascetic, blissfully unaware of the devotee's intentions carried on. But unfortunately, the charm and playfulness, of the beauty unshackled passion. He was overcome by desire. His heart and mind were no longer in resonance. Vishvamitra lost interest in his studies. He wished to unite with her. His mind was clouded by love. Shakuntala was born thus.

The responsibilities of domesticity burdened Vishvamitra. He felt shackled. Love took a backseat. Both the parents went back to their old ways, leaving the child on the banks of river Malini. Vultures, birds and wild animals guarded the baby in wilderness.

Kanva, one day caught sight of the child crying, lying alone, while on his way to perform ablutions. He brought her home and named her Shakuntala, since she was found in the solitude of the forest surrounded by birds. There are three types of fathers; one who gives birth, the other type protects and the third type gives food. Kanva had not given birth to Shakuntala but was a father to her in the complete sense and she was his daughter.

The king was besotted by Shakuntala's beauty and mannerism. He unabashedly talked of his love for her and proposed to marry her by Gandharva rites. But the lady had reservations. Her father was away and there was no one around for her marriage.

DUSHANTA MARRIES SHAKUNTALA

Dushanta was a wise man. He explained thus; every human being is the master of his destiny and his being for which he needs no permission from others. There are eight kinds of marriages sanctioned by dharma–Brahma, Daiva, Arsha, Prajapatya, Asura, Gandharva, Rakshasha and Paishacha. The Gandharva and Rakshasha form is permissible for kshatriyas. This was the law given by Manu, the great philosopher. In Gandharva form of marriage, no ceremonies and no relations are present. Groom and the bride marry each other, out of love and willingly. The king further cajoled the shy maiden, into marrying him, for their mutual love for each other.

Enlightened by the wisdom imparted, Shakuntala agreed to unite with him in marriage without her father's presence or permission. But she wished that the son born of the union would be the future king, to which Dushanta readily agreed. He promised to make her his wife and take her to his kingdom with full honour.

Both of them married according to Gandharva rites and the king set out on his journey back home, promising to send his army to escort her back to the palace, with full honour assigned to a wife. On his way, back to the palace, Dushanta started worrying about Kanva's anger, on the turn of events that had taken place in his absence.

Instead, Kanva was very happy. With age, wisdom and divine sight, he knew everything without being told. He discoursed thus; a marriage between two willing, desirous adults without rites and without mantras is best for Kshatriyas. This act of union is in line with Justice and there is nothing to be ashamed of. Dushyant is best among men, brave and just. The pious father wished his daughter well in life. He blessed her with all his heart. He hoped that the union resulted in the birth of a son, who would be a great soul, mighty, fearless and irresistible. He further wished that the prestige and pride of Puru lineage be upheld in the generations to come.

BIRTH OF BHARATA

Soon Shakuntala gave birth to a son of immense energy, generosity and strength. Kanva and the priests in the hermitage, performed all the rites at the time of birth. From early childhood only the boy showed all signs of a future warrior. He would be seen sporting with lions, tigers, boars and buffaloes near the hermitage. The inhabitants called him Sarvadamana, meaning one who subjugates everyone.

Kanva had observed the boy's progress, his brilliance all these years. He exhibited all the qualities of a prince apparent. The child was only six but extraordinary for someone his age. The rishi made all the arrangements to send the boy and his mother away, to the father.

Time had come for Shakuntala, to go and live with her husband. A married woman's stay longer than stipulated at her paternal home raised questions about her virtue and character. After paying obeisance to the king, she introduced the king's son to him and requested him to accept him as the heir apparent as promised at the time of marriage.

On being told the king recalled the entire episode of his marriage to Shakuntala. But surprisingly he pretended not to remember anything and instructed her to go away with her son. The lady felt humiliated in the presence of the entire assembly and stood paralysed and immobile with shock. Her eyes turned charcoal red, reflecting her anger and lips quivered in disgust. Years of austerities and learning prevented her from losing her cool. She blatantly accused the king of lying.

She was outraged at his insolence. She lashed out at him. A person who knows the truth but acts ignorant is a sinner. While committing a sin man thinks that there are no witness, but there is goodness, the god in every heart, who is the mute witness. Then also there is the sun, moon, wind, fire, earth, day, night and Yama that knows a man's exact deeds. When we lie, we degrade our own soul and even our heart does not forgive us. Shakuntala further admonished the king thus.

"I am your wife and need to be treated with respect and honour. A wife bears children who carry forward the man's lineage. She looks after the house and her husband. She is a faithful friend to him in solitude, a mother in sufferings and a father in religious acts. She always stands by him in adversities' and is a source of strength and inspiration in trying times. A man's soul is passed on to his children.

When he looks at his children, he looks into his mirror image and is as over joyous as the sight of no other living thing can give him. A wife is an epitome of love, joy and virtue. Let's not abuse her. She urged the king to embrace his son whom she bore and who looked up to his father with utmost love and affection".

In grief Shakuntala lost control over self. She was full of remorse. First, it was her mother Maneka who had abandoned her after birth for no fault of hers. Similarly the king too refused to acknowledge his relationship with her and their son. It was the king himself, who had approached her in the forest, when he was on a hunting expedition. She felt deceived all over again for the second time in life, that too by her own relations. But wise that she was, she quickly recovered from her grief and offered to leave for her hermitage again but humbly urged the king to accept their son as their own.

With a heavy heart the king continued with the charade of ignorance. In response to Shakuntala's rejoinder he retaliated, "You were born of your mother Menaka's lust, desire and arrogance for Vishvamitra. Your father Vishvamitra was a kshatriya but his unholy craving for fame and omniscience led him to the path of celibacy. But if as you claim you are the daughter of illustrious Maneka and great ascetic warrior Vishvamitra, your rudeness and disrespect for me, in the presence of the entire assembly belie your claim. You are dressed shabbily and don't appear to bear any semblance to your illustrious parents. You talk like someone from the lower rungs of society and appear to be born out of lust and passion. Your son too appears to be too big for someone who is six years old as you claim him to be. Kindly take yourself and him away from me and my palace".

Shakuntala on hearing the king's odious words lambasted, "It is easier to see and criticize others faults however small, than our own, no matter how big. My parentage is much superior to yours. My mother was a noblewoman in her own right and my father a learned warrior. I have deep knowledge of the universe. A good human being never demeans anyone. An evil person talks ill of others but an honest one feels pain at doing so. Good human beings always respect and honour the wise but the evil try to berate him for solace. Those who seek no evil in others live happily. It is absolutely ridiculous to see the evil project the wise ones as evil. A man who rejects the paternity of his own child shall be damned. Children should never be abandoned. It is said that one can have children from one's wife and if not possible, adopt, or have from other women through surrogacy. Children inspire righteousness in men and are a source of happiness and pleasure.

It is our duty to protect our children, that in turn helps us in safeguarding ourselves and truth. It is as important as all the achievements and tasks one performs in life. There is no religion or religious text higher than truth; no evil greater than falsehood.

Truth is the ultimate oath. Don't violate your own words, the oath you had taken before your marriage to me. O king! Unite with truth and not falsehood. Whether you accept your son or not, he shall still be the king of the earth, blessed by the universe." Having said these harsh but true words, Shakuntala prepared to leave. Dushanta's heart urged him, to accept his wife and son, for they would leave forever. His child, his son was a part of him, his mirror image. The mother only gives birth to the child but it is the father who is the creator of embryo.

The king addressed the assembly thus; I feigned ignorance to clear suspicion in the minds of my people about the authenticity and truth regarding my son's birth and parentage. I wanted people to understand that the union was pure and the child was outcome of my love for my wife and not driven by lust and passion. I did not want any doubts regarding his lineage in future. The king affectionately embraced his son and wife according to full religious rites and law. The son was instated as heir apparent, and named Bharata.

Bharata grew up to be just and invincible. He ruled wisely and brought neighbouring kings and kingdom under control. People called him Sarvabhouma meaning sovereign of the world. He anointed Kanva as his advisor and made lots of offerings as alms. All the other kings, that followed were said to belong to the Bharata lineage. Universe is said to be self created. From the universe, arose lots of illustrious beings.

One of them is Daksha, who is said to be the grandfather of the world. Narada, taught the philosophy of Sankya meaning salvation. Daksha was the father to daughters, granddaughters, sons and grandsons. Non living entities justice and time are supreme. Manu is the father of all human beings. Every race, be it of ascetics or warriors or any other, have known to descend from Manu. It is known that there have been till date fourteen Manus, each presiding over the circle of birth, death and recreation

Ila, an ardent follower of warrior race gave birth to Pururava. He was a brave warrior and ruled over many islands. But valour brings arrogance. He showed no respect for the learned Brahmins. His power, arrogance and avarice brought about his downfall. Surprisingly, his descendants learnt from his mistakes. One of his illustrious grandsons Nahusha was extremely wise and devoted to truth. He treated all kshatriyas, Brahmins, Gandharvas the singing community and even others like Nagas and demons with lots of respect. Only the evil were treated with contempt.

One of Nahusha's known son was Yayati. He was just like his father invincible and benevolent. When time came for his sons to descend the throne he requested all of them to allow him to continue to rule lest he retired and became old and worthless. Yadu and other sons refused to comply except for Puru. Yayati continued to rule like any other king, whereas his son Puru grew wise and old in the sidelines assisting his father. But time takes its own course and eventually time ran out for Yayati. He instated Puru on the throne and the lineage came to be known as Puru's in future after the wise old Puru.

THE RISE OF PURU

There was a power struggle between the good and the demons. Even the demons had grown very powerful. The good ones appointed Angirasa as their advisor while the demons had the wise Kavya Ushanas. The two learned wise men could not stand the sight of each other. Both the warring sides killed each others members.

To add to the misery Ushanas with his knowledge and learning, cured most of the injured and sick but on the other hand Angirasa though extremely learned had no knowledge of treating the ill with the herbs that could bring back the sick into life.

In misery, with great hope the ailing went to Kacha, Angirasa's eldest son. They requested him to get the knowhow of curing the ill from Kavya Ushanas. On the other hand Ushanas always protected the demons. He had a beautiful daughter Devyani.

Having been honoured, Kacha went to Kavya Ushanas. He introduced himself as the grandson of Brihaspati and requested the learned one to take him in his tutelage. The youngster agreed to take vows of celibacy as long as he was under his preceptor's guidance. Kavya accepted his disciple with respect for he was the son of great rishi Brihaspati.

Both the preceptor and disciple had great respect for each other. Kacha worshipped both the tutor and his daughter with great reverence and devotion. He adhered vehemently to his vows of celibacy. But Devyani who was at the peak of her youth found love in Kacha.

Unfortunately, in the meantime, the demons had managed to unearth Kacha's identity. Enraged and not wanting to impart the knowledge of medicinal herbs they almost killed him when he had gone to the forest alone, one day. Devyani was the first one to notice his absence in the evening, for he would light the fire after sunset.

With the knowledge of precious herb sanjivani, Kavya Ushanas brought the almost dead Kacha back to life. But the venom of the demons did not subside at this. On getting an opportunity they again pounded the young man to pulp. In the meantime the demons engaged the preceptor to a wine drinking session. In the company of demons, Kavya had got addicted to liquor. Again on not seeing Kacha around for some time, Devyani went out in search of him. She found him almost left for dead by the demons.

She urged her father to treat his dying disciple. Unfortunately Kavya was in no position to treat the wounded Kacha in his highly intoxicated state. He urged his daughter to accept the fate that had befallen on the skilled, intelligent and loving disciple. But Devyani was a girl in love. She was not willing to give up so easily. She threatened to die on the same pyre as Kacha. Provoked the father tried healing the badly wounded Kacha. Kacha was disillusioned with Kavya's current orientation as he remembered everything on regaining consciousness. The learned man's brilliant life had been overshadowed by demonic ways. Excessive drinking was killing him.

Devyani's life was at cross roads. Her father and the man she loved were dying a slow death. There was no one she had to live for. For the love of his daughter and his dormant high values which scorned the death of a knowledgeable one if at all preventable, Kavya first treated Kacha and then shared with him the knowledge of the medicinal herb in treating the ill.

This was for the first time in his lifetime that he had shared such invaluable information with someone. He saw in Kacha his own son, for it is only to a child one imparted such a rich legacy. Kacha, in turn with his new found secret knowledge treated the ailing and aging, Kavya who was just like a father to him. Kacha's education under his reverend preceptor was now complete. With all the hardships he had endured to reach the nadir, they had enriched his personality.

He shone like a moon on earth. Kavya blessed him wholeheartedly and advised him to tread on the path of truth alone. Kacha reciprocate the sentiments. He paid rich tributes thus; the place of the preceptor in an individual's life comes on the top most rung of the ladder. The giver of knowledge must always be revered, worshipped and placed on a pedestal in one's heart.

Kavya on the other hand was disgusted with himself. He was highly intoxicated while his disciple laid bleeding and dying for want of treatment. He called upon all the ascetics to abstain from consuming alcohol in future. It robbed a person of his senses and well being. He asked all the demons to accept Kacha and respect him. Kacha was now powerful. He had the power to give life to a dying man. Kacha, continued to serve his preceptor. Finally, the time arrived when he asked permission to leave for home to be with his own people. His vow of celibacy too had concluded.

Devyani in full bloom of youth confessed her love for Kacha; oh brilliant one! Your education under my father is now complete. You are no longer under vows of celibacy. I am deeply in love with you. I am very sure you too love me but your vows till now prevented you from acknowledging it. Marry me with full rites". Kacha was aghast. He was at loss of words. He uttered an almost inaudible apology.

He said, "Your father respects me and I in turn respect him. He is my preceptor and you are his daughter. He looks up to me as a son. Thus, by relation we both are brother and sister. Any notion of marital love would be immoral". Devyani was losing patience with Kacha's denial and arguments.

She argued, "You are my father's preceptor's son and not his own. Kindly feel no guilt. Don't forget my love, affection and devotion for you, all this while you were here". But Kacha was adamant.

He remained within the precincts of lawfulness. He bid her farewell and got ready to leave. He requested her to never to have any hard feelings for him but always remember him as someone who was honest and law abiding. But Devyani was a woman scorned in love. She wished him ill in life in the future. She hoped that all his education bore no fruit and went waste.

But now even Kacha was losing patience with Devyani's immaturity. He retorted," I have always conducted my life righteously and I did no wrong to you. So no ill shall result from your venom. Your anger stems from ill begotten desires and not out of love for me. My knowledge shall always give solace to people in need". Saying this he left with a heavy heart.

The people of his land accepted him wholeheartedly. They profusely thanked his father Angirasa, for sending away his son to the land of demons for their welfare. The wise too had attained the knowledge of medicinal herbs from Kacha and were no longer afraid of confronting the demons.

One day Sharmishta, demon king Vrishaparva's daughter and Devyani were sporting in the forest with their companions. A heavy gust of wind scattered all their clothes in different directions. After emerging from the water everyone picked up the pieces of clothes that came their way. Sharmishta ended up with Devyani's garment. This led to an argument between the two friends. Each ranted about their superior lineage while demeaning the other.

Sharmishta called Devyani the daughter of a beggar who praised the king, her father, and held up his hands for alms while her father was the giver. Devyani rebutted calling her the daughter of a demon. On hearing this the girl lost her cool and pushed Devyani in a well leaving her there to die.

On that fateful day, Nahusha's son Yayati had gone hunting in the forest. His horses were tired and thirsty. He reined them and looked into the well. The sight was mystifying. The well was dry and a beautiful maid was in the well looking distraught and calling for help. She told the king that she was Kavya's daughter who cured the sick and dying with medicinal herbs and her father was unaware of her present plight. The king helped her out and returned to the kingdom.

Still seething in rage Devyani rushed her companion Ghurnika to her father for she herself refused to enter king Vrishaparva's kingdom. On hearing of the fight between the two friends, Kavya came rushing to the forest. He reprimanded his daughter and reminded her that a person himself is responsible for his miseries and happiness.

But out of stubbornness Devyani continued her ranting. She tried inflaming anger in her father by repeating constantly that Sharmishta had called her a beggar's daughter who praised the king for sustenance. Kaavya put in his best to make his daughter see sense. He told her that he was a man of high learning and was appreciated by one and all. Moreover one should never cling to the nasty words uttered by others but cast them off like a snake who casts off his dead skin. True strength lies in forgiveness and reign over anger. To achieve your objectives in life, never befriend anger and hurtful words uttered by others.

But Devyani was the daughter of a learned man. She counter philosophized. "Father I am aware of the fact that anger is weakness and forgiveness is strength. But a wise man should never live in the company of the people with bad intentions. People, who have no respect for their preceptor or talk ill of high birth and good conduct should be shunned. Only the weak thrive on the success of their rivals".

Love for his daughter blinded Kaavya. He rushed to the king and blasted. "O King, your people once tried to kill my innocent and humble disciple Kacha. Your daughter insulted my daughter. You are the king of demons. Results of evil actions are manifested in some form or the other like undigested food but may not be visible immediately. I have always lived an honest life without any falsehood. I wish to take leave. But I suggest that you try to find faults in the people around you and reform them rather than overlooking".

Vrishaparva was extremely disturbed at what he had heard. He requested Kavya Ushanas to change his mind and not leave him and his people rudderless. But the angry father was adamant. He wanted his daughter appeased at any cost. The king offered to give away any amount of wealth and goods to Kaavya's daughter. When all that failed the king himself went up to her. Devyani, haughtily demanded that Sharmishta along with her maids be made her slaves after her marriage.

The king sent for Sharmishta. At her father's command she immediately agreed to be at Devyani's bidding. For the welfare of the people of the kingdom, she felt it her duty to prevent Kavya Ushanas from leaving. Devyani was now convinced that knowledge and strength of learning were supreme.

KING YAYATI

Devyani and Sharmishta continued to be companions. But the equation had changed. The mistress was now the maid. Devyani and Sharmishta, one fine day, while frolicking in the forest ran into Yayati. Both of them introduced themselves. Devyani said that she was the daughter of an ascetic and Sharmishta was the daughter of the king but now her maid.

Yayati was intrigued on learning that the king's daughter was a slave. Devyani sermonized that destiny was the ultimate and everyone acted accordingly. When Yayati's turn came he introduced himself as the king and the son of a king. He added that he had acquired vast knowledge when he was young.

Devyani was smitten by Yayati's status and learning. She offered to marry him. Yayati was somewhat aghast at what he had heard. She was a Brahmin and he was a kshatriya. Although all the four classes; Brahmin, kshatriya, vaishya and shudra had evolved from one single entity irrespective a Brahmin was much superior from the rest. An angry kshatriya could kill only a few at a time but an angry Brahmin was capable of eliminating the entire community with his venom in no time.

Yayati did not wish to incur the wrath of a Brahmin by accepting his daughter's proposal. He point blank refused unless and until it had the approval of her father. Fearlessly Devyani went up to Kavya Ushanas and told him that she wished to marry king Yayati, for he was the one who had saved her life when she was pushed into the well by Sharmishta. Kaavya was pleased with his daughter's choice of a brave and valorous husband. He wholeheartedly agreed to bestow her on him.

But Yayati had his own doubts. He was worried that a marriage between a Brahmin and a kshatriya would be considered a sin and the birth of their children would be looked down upon. Kavya allayed the king's doubts. He told him that as long as he loved and respected his wife no evil shall befall on him. But the Brahmin warned the king to not cast a covetous look on the maid Sharmishta who would accompany his daughter after marriage. The marriage between the two stratas was solemnised with full rites.

Separate quarters were assigned to Devyani. Sharmishta lived along with the other maids. In the meantime Devyani gave birth to a lovely radiant son. Sharmistha started feeling envious of her once friend turned foe. She had everything ; a princely husband, children and was the queen herself. Whereas her own youth was waning and as long as she continued to live in the maid's quarter, she would not be able to find a husband of high stature.

With glib words and emotional blackmail Devyani had tricked her. Now she planned to do the same to her. One day on finding king Yayati alone in the groove she went up to him and after initial pleasantries requested him to help her beget a child lest her youth just passed by. The king was aghast. Moreover he had given his word to Devyani's father to be faithful to his wife. The lady counter argued. It would be against laws of nature to not beget a child if one was capable of. Ultimately the children would be Yayati's for a father is the lawful guardian of his children. This act would be righteous since she was but a maid and the children would be his.

With glib argments the king was persuaded. Yayati united with Sharmistha. Both became parents to a son, radiant and healthy. The news of the birth of a son to Sharmishta made Devyani envious. She marched up to her and accused her of indulging in passion and desire arising out of youth. She wished to know the name and lineage of the child's father. "My son is the boon of a radiant and brave man and not a product of passion. His father is a great warrior". Devyani was taken in by the other lady's deception. She believed in what she was being told and carried on with life merrily. With passing time, Devyani had two sons, Yadu and Turvasu while Sharmishta had three radiant ones Druhyu, Anu and Puru. But the former was unaware of the latter's progenies.

But all well kept secrets have strange ways of unfolding themselves. One day while Yayati and Devyani were strolling in the forest they spotted three very handsome children playing. The queen unwittingly remarked that they looked very radiant like the king himself. When she asked them about their parents they looked towards the king and said that Sharmishtha was their mother. Everything fell in place.

In mad fury Devyani went back stomping. She accused Sharmishtha of impropriety and following the law of demons, wherein others belongings were forcibly snatched and not asked for. Without any guilt or remorse Sharmishtha countered every attack bravely and logically.

Then it was the turn of the king to answer questions. To garner support Devyani in anger and humiliation marched out of the king's abode and left to narrate her woes to her father Kaavya. The worried and frightened king too followed her. She ranted thus on seeing her father," the demons have deceived the learned ones who are much superior to them. Evil has triumphed over the good. Sharmishtha has three sons from the king. The king has gone back on his promise to you and crossed over the threshold of faith and trust".

Angry Kaavya accused the king of adultery and committing a sin. In order to save face and his marriage the king passed on the onus to Sharmishtha. He clarified that it was the demon maid who had approached him for the fruition of season. He felt it his duty to comply with the request lest the sin of killing of the embryo lay on his shoulders.

Kaavya was an intelligent man and could not be duped by undue reasoning. "You needed to have taken the permission of your wife. By not doing so you have committed a falsehood, a sin. Youth shall not last forever. It is short. But old age is very long and tortuous. For this act of deceit Devyani, Sharmishta and their sons shall leave you and so shall youth. You will have no choice but to be old and lonely for the rest of your life from now onwards," he countered angrily.

The intensity of the situation hit Yayati like a boulder. Devyani along with Sharmishtha and the sons were leaving not wanting to hear any more lies. He begged them for forgiveness but they refused to listen. Even the sons were following their mothers. Yayati suddenly felt like an old man with no family. He begged his sons to stay back with him.

Yadu the eldest refused saying that he would not like to live in the company of a weak, incapacitated and a cheerless old man. Turvasa the one younger to him refused saying," Old age destroys desire, pleasure, beauty and strength. He did not wish to associate with anyone who was old". The king was mystified at his son's views. He wandered as to the values he would set forth for his subjects, once he was the king. Presumably all of them would be fun loving, indulge in lust and have no respect for relationships.

Sharmishta's son Druhyu was fond of sports like elephant racing, chariot and horse riding and indulged in mindless passion. He did not wish to be associated with his old father. He had no patience to be with an old man who drooled and whose speech slurred with age.

Yayati's heart sank on hearing his sons talk. He loved them dearly. He hoped one day they would realise their folly when their children treated them likewise. But the youngest of the lot Puru was different.

He was humble, kind and co joined with Justice. He accepted the humble request his father was making to his brothers. The goodness in Yayati's heart blessed him. He wished him prosperity and happiness in future. Puru lived by his father's side giving him all his strength, energy and absorbing the cares and whines of old age.

Now Yayati wished to make amends for the transgressions he had made in his youth. With the help of his son Puru he continued to rule wisely and bravely within the precincts of law. All the stratas of society were treated with respect and given protection. He valued every moment of his life for with advancing age he would be incapacitated. Finally when he had lived his life to the fullest time came bidding. He passed on the reigns to Puru.

KING PURU

But there were voices of dissent at Puru's instatement on the throne. The Brahmins and the subjects questioned the king's decision. Logically the eldest son Yadu was to be the lawful inheritor. But Yayati was adamant and firm on his decision. "My older sons have no respect for me, my decisions and welfare. But the youngest of the lot Puru, respects my words. He has concerns for my old age".

He requested the Brahmins to bless Puru and wish him prosperity. Children who show concern for their parents in turn deserve love and affection. The king then left for the forest. Yadu's sons came to be known as Yadavas, Turvasu's were Yavanas, Druhyu's were Bhoja's and Anu's mlecchas. Finally Puru initiated the Pourva lineage.

Yayati himself retired to the forest. He lived a healthy and happy life on fruits, vegetables, practising yoga and meditating. It was complete bliss, heaven. He had caste away his disobedient children to the far end of his kingdom, far away from the periphery of his love, affection and care.

One day while asleep the Almighty Rain soaked the great soul. In his sleep, Yayati explained his magnanimous vision of life; there is no point clinging to anger. Let it go. Good deeds and anger can never go hand in hand. The latter always suppresses the former. Saying harsh, cruel and abrasive words to others damage us more than the other person. Goodness and happiness desert us thus and we become awkward bedfellows of evil. An honest and righteous being need to fear no one except for what that transpires behind his back without his knowledge. Let's pay no heed to the cruel words of the wicked even though they corrode the innermost core. The learned never thinks of releasing them back. Compassion pacifies the heart of both the speaker and the listener. Let's not be harsh and honour those who deserve our respect.

But it seemed Yayati had started gloating in his achievements and success had gone to his head. He had developed a gnawing feeling that there was no one on this earth superior to him even the great ascetics and scholars. Just like a learned is more superior to ignorant one, men to animals, Yayati started considering himself above all beings.

Suddenly Yayati got up with a start from his slumber. He felt as though the mighty Rain was reprimanding him for his overbearing thoughts and attributes. He had learnt a lot but not the basic principle of showing respect to all whether superior or of lower rung. For the next few days there was a heavy downpour which was never visible before. Yayati's abode was literally wiped out. This was Rain's justice.

To learn more Yayati moved back from the forest to live among the ascetics who spent their time in mastering philosophy, science, number work and the fine art of warfare. There he met the great Ashtaka. The

Brahmin was curious. Yayati, as brilliant as Sun himself had moved back from the forest to live among his people!

Yayati with all his brilliance dispel his doubts. Like the ocean learning is also unfathomable. But unlike the former happiness, miseries and material wealth has limitations. The secret lies in being happy with whatever one gets in life. The wise never trembles in fear in adversities for they know destiny is playing truant. On earth we lose friends when we lose wealth, but god forsakes us when we trudge on the path of evil. People stop growing when they start revelling in their own achievements. Good ones part way with them and the jackal among men make inroads in their lives. With time age corrodes them physically and evil friends corrode them mentally.

Man is reborn in his own children, even though his mortal body may die and is turned to ash. His good and evil deeds are reflected in his children. The same principle of procreation applies to animals, plants, insects and other living beings. Progeny makes the living being immortal.

Ashtaka was eager to know more. He begged Yayati to carry on with his discourse. Thus went the knowledgeable king. Learning and knowledge should lead us to tranquillity, self control and compassion towards fellow being. But the same knowledge becomes lethal when we use it to defame and demean others. Primary function of learning is to dispel fear. Sacrifices, vows of silence, studying and learning should be carried out not out of fear but to dispel it. All these practises must be carried out willingly to become better human beings and not lead to arrogance and pride.

A learned man always honours the good. The evil does not possess the intelligence of the learned. Learning and austerities are carried out to unite with the good and dispel fear. Finding peace is the ultimate motive.

Ashtaka, was curious to know more. His mind was unravelling the solution to the riddles that puzzled him. His mind had always been in a quandary as to whether it was possible to be noble being a householder. Should mendicants live on hill tops, the Himalayas to come close to truth? Yayati with all his learning and knowledge tried to dispel the doubts that plagued him. A householder too could be sagacious. Freedom from avarice would free his mind and soul. He should treat his guests well and give away all he had after providing for his family in alms.

Ashtaka's thoughts were getting direction. But he was still confused about good deeds being pursued only in the precincts of forests and hills and not in the cities. Place of residence was not important. A true honest person was one who had conquered desire, sorrow and happiness irrespective of habitat.

In other words, an ascetic freed himself mentally from all attachments; material and emotional. He was in rigid control of his senses. He just possessed enough to survive. Eventually he educated not only himself but all the people around him too. A person who is clean not only physically but spiritually too is worthy of worship. He is a true ascetic. He is the one who is indifferent to pain, pleasure, happiness and eats only to live. His main purpose of life is learning and teaching righteous behaviour. Yayati, carried on explaining to Ashataka the true meaning of a sage.

Yayati went on to explain to Ashtaka that he too had become a sage but not in the true sense. The gains from the austerities had turned his head. He felt he was superior to others and was invincible. But Time is a great teacher. Yayati had to move back from the forest, full of bliss, with animals, flowers and plants back to the town to live among righteous people.

Ashtaka immediately offered Yayati to come and live with him in his forest. Yayati, flatly refused saying that one should never accept gifts unless the person was a ascetic who maintained no fire all his life and lived on begging. Even when one is stuck with adversities one should not accept gifts for they bring no welfare. Fruits of hard work are best enjoyed by the person himself and it is cruel to take them away from him. A person walking on the path of righteousness should out of greed desist from being mean.

All this while another illustrious scholar Vasumana had come and joined Ashtaka and Yayati. He had lots of respect for the aging king. He offered to share his abode in the forest and asked Yayati to pay a perfunctory price or accept it as a gift, since the king did not want to share other's merits. Yayati profusely blessed the boy for his magnanimity but refused the offer. saying he would derive no pleasure from surroundings that did not belong to him.

Yayati was all praise for king Shibi. He was the one who had used all his riches for the welfare of others keeping none for himself. Yayati too had given away all his wealth to the austere Brahmins. Goodness on earth prevails because of the good deeds of its inhabitants. Truth is the guiding principle. The learned swear by this principle.

Yayati's illustrious son Puru carried forward his lineage. Puru's sons, grandsons, great grandsons were like him. Dushanta, the eldest grandson married Shakuntala and became parents to Bharata. It is from him the Bharata dynasty took roots. Bharata had three wives and nine sons. He did not find any of his sons talented and good enough for the throne. So he adopted professor Bharadvaja's son Bhumanyu and instated him. Bharata's son Vitatha was adopted by Bhumanyu. Bhumanyu's progenies ruled the earth wisely. They performed many horse sacrifices and ruled the subjects in accordance with law.

BHARATA'S LINEAGE

Bharata's lineage continued to flourish through, sons, grandsons and great grandsons. Bhumanyu's eldest son Suhotra was the king. But it was during the times of his great grandson Samvarana that a disaster struck the kingdom. Famine and disease plagued the subjects. There was total chaos and devastation. To add to the woes the kingdom was attacked by the enemies none other than the Panchalas. Panchalas were the cousins of Samvarana.

King Samvarana fled with wife, sons, friends and advisors after the Panchalas defeated him and took control over his kingdom. The Bharatas found shelter on the banks of river Indus. The entourage lived there for many years to come. The radiant Vashishtha became their chief officiating priest. With his guidance and help they again regained their kingdom back after lots of inhuman struggle. The descendant of Puru was again reinstated. Samvarana had a son Kuru who later ascended the throne. Kuru was a wise man. He was the one who made the place Kurukshetra famous with his presence. It was initially called Kurujangala. The Bharata lineage.

Bharata's great grandson Pratipa had three sons; Devapi, Shantanu, Bahlika.

Devapi became an ascetic and retired to the forest. Shantanu was anointed the king. He was sagacious who alleviated people's pain and suffering, hence Shantanu meaning peaceful. Shantanu married a damsel Ganga, on the banks of that very river and had a son Devavratha fondly called Bhishma. Bhishma, urged the king his father, to marry Satyavati, since he was besotted by her beauty and mannerism.

Satyavati had, had a son Krishna Dvaipayna, through Parashar before marriage to Shantanu. After marriage she had two more sons; Vichitravirya and Chitrangada. After Chitrangada's death Vichitravirya became the king. Vichitravirya married two sisters; Amba and Ambalika, daughters of king of Kashi. Unfortunately, he died young without any heir. Satyavati was now a worried mother.

Her son was dead, leaving behind no child to continue the lineage. All she could think of was to summon her other son Krishna Dvaipayna who was a confirmed ascetic scholar to help her continue the Dushanta's lineage. In spite of his vows, Krishna accepted his mother's request. Thus were born Dhrithrashtra, Pandu and Vidhur.

Later in life Dhritrashtra had lots of sons, the most known and illustrious were; Duryodhana, Duhshasana, Vikarna and Chitrasena. Pandu had two wives, Kunti and Madri.

One day while on a hunting spree he aimed at something that appeared to be stag. But unfortunately, that was a rishi in his abode with his wife. The dying rishi was furious. He lashed out at Pandu.

He wished, like him, he too left the universe without giving birth to a child. That would be a grave sin. Let the person responsible for this demeanour too faced the same fate, he cursed. It appeared as though the universe too was in connivance with the ascetic. Pandu was incapable of becoming a father.

Kunti, had sons Yudhishthira, Bhima, Arjuna through ascetics who were deep in the world of philosophy and knowledge of warfare. Likewise Madri too had twins' Nakul and Sahdev from a very sagacious ones. Thus Pandu's righteous sons came into being.

Madri died on her husband Pandu's funeral pyre, leaving her twins in the care of Kunti. Kunti along with the Pandavs accompanied by the ascetics went to Hastinapur to seek their rightful share in the kingdom. They were introduced to Vidhur and Bhishma.

Dhritrashtra and his sons did not like Pandavs presence in their lives. They left no stone unturned to eliminate them from the scene. Their cousins would have charred them up in the house of lacquer had Vidhur not intervened and saved them. After an attempt on their life the Pandavs along with their mother did not return to Hastinapur but instead started living a life of anonymity, moving from one town to another.

During their sojourn of anonymity they killed demons Hidimba and Baka in the town of Ekachakra, headed for the capital of Panchala and married Draupadi. Then all of them with their mother returned to Hastinapur, their very own country. Their sons were equally valorous. Yudhishthira had Prativindhya, Vrikodara had Sutasoma, Arjuna had Shrutakirti, Nakula had Shatanika and Sahdev had Shrutakarmana.

In a swayamvara wherein a bride chooses her own groom, Yudhishthira married Devika, who was of the Shibi lineage, and had a son Youdheya. In a Viryashulka the bride marries a person who exhibits valour. Bhima got Baladhara, daughter of king of Kasha. He had a son Sarvaga. Arjun married Subhadra, Vasudev Krishna's sister, in Dvaravati. Both had a son Abhimanyu.

Nakul married Karenumati from Chedi and had a son Niramitra. Sahadeva married Vijaya, in a swayamvara, and had a son Suhotra. Bhim also had a son Ghatotkacha from demon girl Hidimbi. Abhimanyu married Uttara, daughter of king of Virata. She gave birth to a premature, stillborn child. But miraculously once in the arms of grandmother Kunti, the child cried out aloud. Everyone was astonished.

Vasudev named him Parikshit meaning extinct, for he was born in a lineage that was almost taking its last breath. Parikshit had the illustrious son Janemajaya through wife Madravati. Through

Vapushtama, he had sons Shatanika and Shanku. This is the Puru lineage in totality.

RISE OF SHANTANU

King Shantanu was righteous and valorous. He had a number of horse sacrifices to his credit. He along with many ascetics once went to pay homage to Brahma by the banks of river Ganga. A very beautiful damsel by the name of Ganga appeared out of wilderness. The king was awestruck by her beauty. He continued looking at her unabashed. Ganga too went away thinking of the handsome youth.

Once back home the lady went to sleep thinking of the king. In her dreams she visualised little children wishing to be born through her. She was pure and they wanted her to be their mother. Ganga got up with a start. With the passage of time she forgot about the incident and carried on with the rituals.

King Pratipa, Shantanu's father was devoted to the welfare of his subjects. He would come and spend days on the banks of river Ganga and meditate. One day Ganga too happened to came and sit by the right side of the meditating king. The king saw the divine beauty full of purity sitting by his side. He felt as though goodness was hinting at something. The king requested her to be his daughter in law.

Ganga gladly accepted the offer. She felt privileged to be married in the Bharata dynasty. It was the synonym with righteousness. But she was a proud woman with lots of self respect. She asked the king to not ever question her heritage or her moral standings. On her part she promised that she would always work for the welfare of her husband and make him happy.

King Pratipa though a valorous warrior had begotten a son after lots of prayers. He was named Mahabhisha. The king called him Shantanu. Shantanu was skilful and became a great archer. He loved hunting. He was devoted to righteous conduct at the same time. Eternal happiness and peace comes with one's own good deeds. Pratipa instated Shantanu on the throne and departed to the forest. Shantanu and Ganga were married.

The king was besotted by her beauty. But Ganga made it amply clear that she would tolerate no harshness in speech or actions from him. That she would act on her own accord and tolerate no interference in her day to day activities. The king would be able to enjoy the pleasure of her love and company as long as he acted appropriately within the precincts of self respect. Shantanu agreed wholeheartedly.

The king abided by his promise. So did the queen. Her conduct, beauty, generosity and qualities were above board. The king was no less radiant. Unfortunately for the couple their children were born still without any trace of life except for one. In order not to hurt her husband the queen quietly went and bestowed the children to river Ganga with a heavy heart.

Likewise the king too refrained from asking. But he was unaware of the reasons. His mind too was in turmoil as to why his wife abandoned his children. Her conduct till now had been impeccable with no place for doubt.

Fortunately the eighth child was normal and alive. Ganga was overjoyed. But by now the king had lost his patience. He angrily went up to his wife and asked her to stop her evil ways and like the rest not abandon the newborn. Ganga was unhappy and shocked at her husband's accusation. All this while she had only thought of his happiness and welfare. Instead he doubted her intentions. This was not love, she thought to herself. She decided to part ways with Shantanu. And on him doubting her integrity, she discoursed thus;

Children are Universe's gift to man. He is their father. We on earth are just the medium to bring them to life. It is Nature who decides the duration of their stay on earth. Your children died at the time of birth only and were freed of all the sufferings one has to undergo. Consider yourself lucky to have fathered eight children. Call the eighth one Gangadatta.

Before leaving she told him the secret she had nursed for so long. She was king Jhanua's daughter. There was professor Vashishtha whose hermitage was by the side of mount Meru. The place was a heaven populated by deer, birds and flowers. In the forest Vashishta's only means of sustenance was the milk of his cow besides the fruits. The cow grazed in the forest throughout the day. One day the cow did not return. Vashishtha was worried. He looked for her all around. He realised that he had seen strangers in the forest, close to his hermitage. The riddle of his missing cow fell in place. The sage was furious. Out of greed the intruder had taken away his cow that too without his permission. The cow's milk had medicinal properties. They wanted it for their friend Jahnavi who was king Jahnu's daughter. Jahnavi refused to accept the gift that had been stolen.

Trespassers were wise and righteous. They realized their mistake. Meekly all of them went up to the enraged owner. The sage mellowed down with their apology. But he said that repentance alone would not undo the wrong they had done. Experiencing pain makes us realize our follies better. He wished that they had no offspring hence devoted their lonely life for the welfare of others. That would be retribution.

When Jahnavi learnt about it she felt sad and agitated. Her friends had stolen the cow for her. Unwittingly she too was a part of the conspiracy. Along with the them she too would have to pay for this transgression of justice. With the passage of time she realised the Vashishta's curse had taken a toll on her and her family. Her seven sons were born without any traces of life giving her immense pain. The youngest one Gangadatta went celibate later in life. Having narrated the account Ganga along with her son left. Gangadatta came to be known as Bhishma. He even surpassed his illustrious father Shantanu in good qualities.

KING SHANTANU AND HIS TIMES!

King Shantanu like his name was a peaceful man. In spite of that he had unsurpassable strength. He was righteous and quite detached from wealth and desire. With such a soul on the throne all the other kings and their subjects were free from fear, sorrow and worries. Brahmins were the scholars, teachers and guides. They were maintained by the royal warriors. Kshatriyas in turn were served by Vaishyas. Shudras served all classes.

Shantanu lived in Hastinapur the capital of the Kurus. One day the king went and sat by the side of river Ganga for meditation. He realised that the flow of the water of Bhagirathi had been obstructed by a volley of arrows. The usually free flowing Ganga's waters were somewhat shallow. The youth who had performed the feat was radiant and handsome. He had a bow and arrow. With his skilful archery he had chequered the flow of Ganga's course. On seeing the king the youth disappeared. All these years the king had never seen his son except at the time of birth. He suspected the youth to be his own son.

He prayed to the mighty Ganga to help him recognise and unite with his son. As though even goodness wanted the wise one to unite with his son, his estranged wife Ganga appeared before him. He had not met her for years, since she had left him. It took the king a while to recognise the aging lady who was once his wife. Both of them greeted each other respectfully. The king wished to unite with his son after so many years of separation. Ganga agreed to the proposal wholeheartedly. With a heavy heart she sent her son to be with his father.

The boy was adept in Philosophy and Art of warfare. He was tutored by Vashishtha himself. He was a supreme archer. He had the blessings of both good and demons. He had trained under none other than Parashurama. Parashurama was invincible with unfathomable knowledge of weapons and warfare. The boy's persona was wholesome befitting kings.

Shantanu very gratefully accepted his son from Ganga. Both of them, the father and son marched up to the capital of the radiant Bharata lineage. The king instated Bhishma on the throne. Both the them enjoyed a great camaraderie. Through his conduct Bhishma won the affection of his people, the courtiers and his father.

One day Shantanu happened to sit in the boat of a beautiful fisherwoman while crossing river Yamuna. She was a ravishing beauty with great mannerism and smile. Her aura was extremely infectious. She told Shantanu that she was the daughter of the king of the fisherman's tribe. It was on the instructions of her father that she plied the boat.

The king wished to make her his wife. He went up to her father and asked for her hand. The father was overjoyed at the proposal from the king. But he had his reservations. He wanted the son from his daughter to be the future king.

But Shantanu was not prepared for that. He rejected the proposal outright and came back to his kingdom with a heavy heart still thinking of the damsel and entrenched in pain and sorrow that love brings. Bhishma on his part was perturbed by his father's behaviour. He always appeared sad and lost in thoughts. The functioning of the kingdom ran very smoothly. All the vassal kings were under control. He could not fathom the cause of his father's anguish.

Certain unknown fears were giving Shantanu sleepless nights. He was proud of his son and never doubted his capabilities. But impermanence of life made him insecure. Bhishma was his only son. What if he was killed in the battle field! His lineage would come to an end and so would his kingdom! He wondered if he would ever be at peace with himself if that were to happen. On learning the reasons of his father's pain, the wise son set out to find a solution. The boy knew that there was something more to the entire truth his father had narrated.

He consulted an old advisor of Shantanu who was his constant companion. The old man solved the riddle. He disclosed the condition imposed by the fishermen king. Bhishma went on his own to ask for the fisherman king's daughter hand. He gave the man his word that his precondition for marriage would be accepted unconditionally and that he allowed his daughter to marry his father. He promised never to sit on the throne after his father's death.

But the man's greed knew no bounds. He was still not done. He went on with his glib narrative; Satyavati my daughter comes from a warrior's lineage. Many learned men asked for her hand. But the Bharata king is most suited for her. He expressed full faith in Bhishma's words for he was devoted to righteousness and truth but had doubts whether in future his children would honour his word. Bhishma immediately understood at what the man was hinting at. For the sake of his father's happiness he took a vow that he would be celibate all his life.

BHISHMA THE INVINCIBLE

Bhishma invited his stepmother Satyavati to accompany him to the kingdom of Hastinapur. Shantanu learned about the vow his son had taken for his happiness. He was overwhelmed with love and respect. He blessed him and wished that he would be able to conquer the invincible death.

Satyavati bore Shantanu a valorous son Chitrangada. He was brave and wise. Another son Vichitravirya graced the couple. He was a great archer. Bhishma in turn had lots of respect for his mother Satyavati. With the passage of time Shantanu left for the final journey. Chitrangada graced the throne.

Chitrangada once had a duel with the king of Gandharvas in the fields of Kurukshetra. The battle raged for three years. Unfortunately the rival king used deception on the field. The Kuru heir never returned back home. Bhishma performed his funeral rites. He then instated Vichitravirya the younger one on the throne. Bhishma acted as his philosopher and guide. The King in turn had immense respect for his older brother who was wise and noble.

When Vichitravirya was old enough Bhishma with Satyavati's consent set out to find suitable brides for the king. The king of Kashi had organised a swayamvara for his three daughters. Bhishma marched up to Varanasi alone in a single chariot for participation. He carried away the three daughters of the king of Kashi forcibly from the altar while others looked on aghast.

But that was an assembly of young princes and kings from all different states who had come to participate in the swayamvara. They got into their chariots and started raining arrows on the fleeing Bhishma. Then ensued a great battle between one and many. The Kuru sliced off the arrows midway and pierced each enemy with his arrows.

Among the eight types of marriages swayamvara is considered to be of the highest form. The groom takes away the bride forcibly and dares the assembly of suitors along with the father to stop him. This exhibits the charioteer's skill and valour. Even the defeated enemies applauded for the fearsome Bhishma's bravery. But king Shalva was seething with envy. He fired at Bhishma's retreating back and ordered him to stop. This angered Bhishma to no end. He turned around to duel with Shalva. The kings present thronged to witness the duel. In the first round Shalva overpowered Bhishma covering him with a canopy of arrows. Everyone present applauded.

Bhishma was livid. He ordered his charioteer to march up to the king. He wished to kill the insolent king like the king of birds killed the snakes. He used his most powerful weapon to wound Shalva's four horses and then killed the charioteer. Ironically he merely wounded and defeated the warrior. This was no war time but merely a contest.

With great honour Bhishma escorted the three daughters of Kashi king along with him passing through forests, mountains and rivers. In consultation with Satyavati he made arrangements for Vichitravirya's wedding.

Before the wedding the older of the three sisters Amba approached Bhishma. She told him that she had talked to her father about her desire to marry king Shalva of Shouba before the swayamvara and he had agreed to the proposal. Even the groom had accepted her as his wife to be.

Amba wanted Bhishma to rethink before marrying her off to his brother. After the revelation the wise men in the court were consulted. They were of the opinion that Amba be allowed to go back to her father.

Accordingly she left for Kashi and her younger sisters' Ambalika and Ambika married Vichitravirya.

The girls and Vichitravirya enjoyed marital bliss. But it was ill fated. One fine day while still in his youth he left for heavenly abode. Vichitravirya left behind grieving wives and mother. Satyavati along with Bhishma and the daughter in laws performed the funeral rites. Satyavati's father's lust and greed for power had cast a shadow on his own daughter's happiness. The injustice done to Bhishma had backfired.

Satyavati sought solace in prayers and meditation. Once pacified she turned her attention at preserving Shantanu's lineage. Her son had left the throne heirless. She tried to find out ways and means of coming out of the crisis. As always she approached Bhishma for advice.

Satyavati wanted Bhishma to be instated on the throne. Moreover Ambika and Ambilika yearned for children. It would be a sin for the young ladies to not have children. The mother wanted Bhishma to be her grandchildren's father.

Bhishma countered her request by reminding her of his vows of celibacy. It would be against righteousness to disregard them. He would always be truthful and not go back on his word. Abiding by one's word was a religion higher than obeying one's mother. He was willing to give up everything and stand by his vows.

But as always he came to Satyavati's aid and suggested ways out of the crisis. He further elaborated that having children on the woman when her husband was no more was not against the law. Great sage Parasurama had killed kshatriyas to avenge the death of his father. After the mindless killing by Parasurama the widowed kshatriya women had not many valorous men left to give them children. These women went to Brahmins to beget children. This was poetic justice. Wise Brahmins gave birth to brave kshatriya warriors.

Similarly Utathya had a blind son Dirghatama. He was violated when still in his mother's womb by none other than his own uncle, rishi Brihaspati hence was born blind. In spite of the physical shortcomings he was a great scholar. King Bali had requested him to help beget children on his wife. Anga was born to king Bali's wife. Brahmins have been known to father brave kshatriyas. Satyavati's predicament had an answer in Bhishma's disclosure.

ENTERS VEDAVYASA

Satyavati had no choice but to bring forth the secret hidden deep in her bosom; the existence of her son Krishna Dvaipayana. She had borne this son on sage Parashara when she was an ordinary boat plying fisher woman. Taken in by her mystical beauty Parashara had wished to unite with her. Afraid of the Brahmin's wrath she had agreed. Krishna Dvaipayana was born thus. He was illustrious like Parashara himself.

The world knew him as Vedavyasa, as one who classifies the Vedas. He had promised to come to his mother's rescue whenever she was in trouble. Vyasa lived the life of an ascetic, was deep in learning and had freed himself from desires. On learning of Vyasa and his ways of life Bhishma felt that he would be the most appropriate person to be the father of his dead brother, Vichitravirya's children.

Satyavati on gaining Bhishma's approval summoned Vyasa from the forest. Mother and son embraced with pent up emotions, breaking the barriers of years of separation. Vyasa wished to know the reason his mother had summoned him but hoped that all that was required of him would well be within the precincts of laws. Any transgression in righteousness would not be welcome even at the mother's beckoning

Satyavati introduced Bhishma to Vyasa. She told him that he was Vichitravirya's brother from father's side. Accordingly Vyasa was his brother from mother's side. Bhishma was under the vow of celibacy and had promised to renounce the throne at one point of time. Since he adhered strictly to principles, he was in no state to beget children for his dead brother who would rule the kingdom in future. For the welfare of the people of Hastinapur who would be without a king in future, once Bhishma stepped down, Satyavati requested Vyasa to be the father of Vichitavirya's children. She hoped he would honour her and wise Bhishma's word.

For the sake of Dharma, VedVyasa felt it his duty to beget children on his dead brother's behalf. A country too needed a king without which it would be rudderless. No place was safe without a king. Satyavati heaved a sigh of relief on hearing her son's words of assurance. But the ascetic was apprehensive whether Ambika and Ambilika would be able to unite willingly with an rugged Brahmin like himself willingly.

Once one hurdle was over Satyavati resorted to sorting out the next. She explained to her daughter in laws that for the good of the country and to prevent the extinction of Bharata lineage it was important that they beget children from their brother in law who had agreed to help. Both the ladies were aghast at the suggestion. Satyavati allayed their doubts by assuring them that the task was within the precincts of law. With a heavy heart both of them agreed reluctantly for the sake of Satyavati's word and the joys of motherhood.

BIRTH OF DHRITRASHTRA, PANDU AND VIDHURA

Satyavati prayed and organised elaborate feasts for ascetics and guests. On the anointed day Vyasa entered Ambika's chamber in the middle of the night. The lady was terrified on seeing the Brahmin. She had expected her brother in law Bhishma or some other kshatriya for the task. On seeing the unkempt and lean Brahmin she shut her eyes in disgust. Vyasa too was offended with her behaviour.

But he had given his word and had to comply. He told his mother that he had accomplished the task assigned but was afraid that the child born would be without vision like the mother who showed scant respect for the austere ascetic. As prophesied the son born of the union was literally blind as seen from the events that unfolded in the future.

Vyasa encountered a similar situation when he went to Ambalika. The lady went pale with fear on seeing the dark impoverished rishi. Satyavati was accordingly told by her intelligent son that he doubted that the child born would be brave and strong since the mother was timid and weak. Pandu did not prove the rishi wrong even though he was radiant and handsome.

Satyavati on her part had not been successful in salvaging the future of the almost dead Bharata lineage. She out of desperation again asked Ambika to unite with Vyasa. Short sighted that she was, Ambika could not bear to be with the frugal and lean Brahmin. Instead she sent her maid bedecked in finery. When Vyasa entered her chamber the lady paid all due respect. She gained it in return with her noble mannerism and behaviour. She served the sage with love and affection. After spending time with her Vyasa was very happy. He wished to unite with her.

He told her that in future she would give birth to a son who would be deep in knowledge and learning and would be amongst the most intelligent men of the universe. She would no longer be a maid but a mother to a sagacious and powerful son. The son born to her was the illustrious Vidhura who was the virtual king of the Kuru dynasty and had the respect of all the great men in the kingdom. Vidhura epitomised Justice. But what baffled the wise was that Dharma chose to take birth in the womb of a woman considered to be from lower rungs of society.

Vaishampayana narrated the ordeals Mandavya had to undergo who was righteous at the hands of ignorant and delusional. Mandavya was devoted to truth and established in Dharma. Once some thieves with a huge treasure hid in his hermitage trying to evade the royal guards. Since the ascetic was under vows of silence he did not answer any queries. On searching the hermitage they found the thieves and the stolen goods. Out of ignorance the royal guards assumed that that the rishi was in connivance and hence had refused to answer any questions. They rounded up the rishi along with the thieves.

The king ordered all of them to be dumped in an isolated place with no means of survival. The rishi even without food and water did not open up. He continued practising Dharma. The thieves felt ashamed of themselves. The rishi was paying for their sins without complaining. They went up to the king and confessed their guilt.

The king was remorseful. Out of ignorance he had committed the sin of punishing a righteous one. With all humbleness and his advisors in tow he went and asked Mandavya for forgiveness. Mandavya was pacified by the king's sincere apology but suspicions regarding his noble intentions hurt like a thorn. He was known as Animandavya, the needle, to the world. The thieves strongly adhered to Dharma. They respected the righteousness of the rishi. Dharma is exclusive of caste, creed and stature.

The honest ones often wander as to why they are punished for the sins they never commit. In spite of the trials and tribulations they continue to move on the path of truth. Brahma has its own means of vindicating them They continue to be free from avarice and anger. No situation can deprive them of their farsightedness and equability. Children too commit crimes. But they are done out of innocence. Hence their acts are not punishable.

After long the dawn of happiness and sunshine set on the Kuru kingdom. The three brilliant sons Dhritrashtra, Pandu and Vidur graced the kingdom. It appeared as though Satya yug wherein Justice was at its best had set in. Mahabharat is known to have taken place in Dvapara era, third of the four eras.

Kurus prosperity started growing after the debacle the kingdom had faced following Vichitravirya's death. There was an abundance of crops. Traders and artisans flourished. People were happy and law abiding. The neighbouring kings too did not fight with one other but lived happily. There were no wars and no widows. In general there was happiness all around. Under Bhishma's guidance, the state flourished. Righteous conduct was the hallmark, oiling the wheels of the administration of the country.

Right from birth Bhishma took the three nephews under his wing. They studied Philosophy and observed the vows. They were trained in archery, horsemanship, fighting with shields, clubs and swords and fighting on elephant back.

Of the three princes Pandu excelled in archery, Dhritharashtra was the strongest and Vidhura was engrossed in the study of Laws. All three excelled in their respective fields. The once flagging Kuru dynasty was now showing signs of revival. Other neighbouring kings had started talking about them. The kingdom and the princes were bringing fame and name.

Ambika and Ambalika were hailed as the mother of heroes and Hastinapur as the model city, Bhishma epitomised Dharma. Pandu was anointed the king when he came of age. Dhrithrshtra was denied the right even though he was the eldest since he was born blind. Vidhur was born to a Shudra woman. Hence he was denied the right.

DHRITRASHTRA WEDS GANDHARI

Bhishma was in charge of the Kuru dynasty on behalf of his young nephews. He wanted to take the lineage to the zenith with his able guidance and policies. He always worked hard along with Satyavati and Krishna Dvaipayna to keep the flag hoisted even in trying times. The time had arrived to further propagate the dynasty. Bhishma engaged with king Subala and Yadavas and asked for their daughters hand in marriage for his nephews. The girls came from good families and were well protected. He consulted Vidura.

Vidura had unwavering faith in Bhishma's good intentions and capability. He stood by his decision. Subala's daughter Gandhari was young and beautiful. Bhishma wished his nephew Dhrithrashtra would marry Gandhari. He got the message conveyed to her father Subala.

Subala was initially aghast at the suggestion of his daughter marrying a blind prince but considering the famous and noble lineage of the groom he agreed reluctantly. Gandhari like her father initially had reservations. But with time she reconciled to the situation and started wearing a band on her eyes to express her solidarity and integrity for her future husband. Father Subala and her brother Shakuni saw her off with lots of wealth.

PANDU WEDS KUNTI AND MADRI

The chief of Yadu dynasty was Shura. He was Vasudev Krishna's father. Shura's eldest sister Pritha had been adopted by Kuntibhoja. Kuntibhoja had no children of his own. This was an act of love and friendship. She was called Kunti by her father. The girl received lots of love and affection at her father Kuntibhoj's home. Kunti as a young woman was very beautiful and attractive. Youth made her transgress. An encounter with a valiant ascetic made her lose control over self. As a result she gave birth to an equally valorous son. The child exhibited all the qualities of a warrior. He came to be known as Karna.

The consequence of her act of immaturity frightened her to no end. At the time of birth she put the child in a basket and set it afloat with a heavy heart. Accidently the boat was spotted by Adhiratha, a charioteer. He took the child home to his wife Radha. Radha was overjoyed. She had no children of her own.

The husband and wife named him Vasushena, meaning riches. The child was the most precious being of their life. Kunti was a maiden again to the outside world. Her son grew up in the charioteer's household. He was a brave and natural warrior. He would practise endlessly with passion the use of weapons. Once the boy came across a Brahmin who asked him for alms. He had nothing to give but the only armour and earrings he had on his person. He did so without a second thought. The amazed Brahmin blessed him profusely. He wished that Karna in future become an infallible warrior and supreme among the bravest. Vasushena now came to be known as Karna Vaikartana.

Kuntibhoja arranged a swayamvara wherein the bride selects a groom from among numerous suitors for his beautiful daughter. He wanted her to move on in life. Lots of princes participated. Pandu, the handsome and valorous was the one chosen by Kunti. Kuntibhoja's daughter and Pandu were married with pomp. Bhishma and Pandu then fixed an alliance with the king of Madra. Madri, the king's daughter was married off to Pandu, in lieu of lots of riches.

Pandu then set out to conquer his neighbours and bring in their riches and people for the welfare of Hastinapur. King Darva though valorous had made lots of enemies. He was the first one to be decimated. His treasury, armies and transport were seized. Next in line was king of Videha. After a long period of fame Shantanu's lineage was revived. Kings who in bad times had robbed the Kurus were now forced to pay tributes to them.

Bhishma continued to remain the guiding force. Pandu in turn made offerings to his mother Ambalika, uncle Vidhura and Bhishma. His subjects were happy and proud of his achievements. After his sojourn of the earth, subjugating and conquering, he was given a hero's welcome. His brother Dhrithrashtra performed horse sacrifices and gave alms to the poor. In general the Kuru dynasty was at its nadir.

Attacking and conquering took a toll. Pandu in future saw no good in it. The attractiveness of war no longer thrilled him. After much contemplation he left the kingdom in the care of his brother Dhrithrashtra and Bhishma.

Madri and Kunti accompanied him to the forest. His maintenance and upkeep was looked after by Dhrithrashtra. He lived like the king of the forest, clad in armour, accompanied by his wives, merry making and hunting.

In the meantime, Bhishma got Vidhura married to the daughter of king Devaka. The girl had a shudra mother like Vidhura. She was virtuous and comely. Vidhura had children from his wife who were humble, virtuous and no less than him in good qualities.

Gandhari, Dhrithrashtra's wife was the mother to lots of valorous sons. They were strong and valorous like their father and had the strength of lots of strong warriors collectively. After Kunti delivered her son, Gandhari became restless. Although heavily pregnant there were no signs of her children.

Out of frustration one day she started squeezing her stomach. The process started. She gave birth to lot of valorous sons and a daughter Duhshala. They were all born through the process of tissue culture.

Dhrithrashtra had a Vaishya maid in attendance. She too gave him a wise son Yuyutsu of mixed lineage. In short all his boys were great charioteers, skilled in battle and radiant in knowledge. When they all attained manhood they were married off to equally brilliant girls. His daughter Duhshala was married to King Jayadratha.

PANDU BECOMES AN ASCETIC

Pandu lived a very lavish life in the forest with lots of attendants in tow. One day he went out hunting and targeted a deer. Unfortunately, it was a rishi Kindama with his wife, whom he mistook for a deer, in the dense forest. The arrow went right through the rishi. The dying rishi could not but reprimand Pandu, for his lustful behaviour. He found Pandu's act evil, sinful and deprived of reason.

Pandu he said came from a noble family and his act was definitely not in keeping with his lineage. His act was absolutely cruel. Pandu was unfazed by the criticism. He clarified his stand. He said that he was a king, a warrior. Whenever a kshatriya saw an enemy, he shot. It was not him but the sage who was deceived. Killing the enemy was his Duty. To him deer and enemy are the same. Both are killed with deceit.

To validate his action, he cited the example of rishi Agasthya who sacrificed every deer of the forest and offered them to the gods. Kindama counter argued. He felt taking the enemy unawares was against the principles of law. Both the parties had to be in a state of preparedness

But Pandu was of a very different opinion. To him, killing only required strength and an arrow. The rishi reminded the king of his duties. It involved killing those who had abandoned a life of righteousness and were engaged in committing a sin. Killing an innocent and helpless one was cruel. He was a simple, honest sage who lived on fruits and roots. He had done no wrong. Injuring an innocent one backfires. That would be the king's punishment. He too shall like him leave the world without an heir, cursed Kindama. Desire, lust and avarice shall be his nemesis. Having said all this, the rishi succumbed to his injuries.

Pandu realized his folly. He plunged in grief. He was a broken man and not the confident Kshatriya who had conquered the earth. The death of an innocent, childless Brahmin at his hands shook him. The dying one's curse kept haunting him.

Even his father out of arrogance and lust for pleasure had hunted a lot of innocent ones. It was their curse that killed him young without leaving behind a child. Pandu and his brothers were born of Krishna

Dvaipayna who was very thoughtful and dharma abiding. In spite of his noble parentage he had plunged low. Fear of impending death owing to follies committed unsettles even the bravest. Pandu felt taking birth in a noble family alone did not warrant the path of righteousness. He wished to appease the self created Universe and seek salvation for the sins committed.

First and foremost he sent a word to his family in Hastinapur that he had decided to denounce worldly pleasures and riches and along with his two wives would live like a hermit for the rest of his life in the forest. Now he no longer needed the royal trappings, the chariots and the attendants. All were sent back to the kingdom. There was grief, a death like remorsefulness in Hastinapur.

But Pandu felt freed from bondage and vice. From then on he was no longer the illustrious prince of an illustrious dynasty. He was an ascetic living on roots and fruits with his head shaved. The foot of the tree was his abode and he had detached himself from worldly pleasures and miseries. At times he went to sleep on an empty stomach when he got no food from begging. He had unshackled himself from the trappings of all material belongings. Fear of death no longer frightened him. He decided not to use his virility for self defence or subduing others.

Kunti and Madri too accompanied Pandu in his retirement to the forest. As wives this was their duty. His brothers' Dhritarashtra and Vidhura were aghast and taken aback by the sudden turn of events. They grieved for his hardships in the forests without luxuries, crown and family. Living on alms offered he travelled through the mountains and plains endlessly halting now and then to rejuvenate. He was protected by the villagers and great rishis who were the fellow travelers. Pandus new abode was Shatashringa, the beautiful mountain with hundred peaks.

BIRTH OF PANDAVS

By now he was a hardcore ascetic, devoted to the welfare of others, in complete control of his senses and without pride or ego. He was one amongst the many ascetics with whom he travelled. Pandu had discharged all his duties and debts but one. As a noble man he had been kind to his fellow beings, practised austerities and had extensively But owing to his shortcomings till date he had not been able to discharge his debt towards his ancestors. He did not have any children. And if he were to die without a progeny his lineage would come to an end. He himself was born of the great sage Krishna Dvaipayna.

He was advised to continue his lineage in the same way he had come to the universe. That would be in tune with laws of Nature. His offsprings would be intelligent like him only. It would be a great source of happiness which no other accomplishment would give.

Now Pandu had a difficult task at hand. Since his own powers of procreation were negligible and the desire to be a parent keen, he talked to his wives into motherhood through illustrious ascetics. He felt as though he was being punished for his cruelty and viciousness towards Kindama who had left the world craving for a progeny. Learned that he was, he educates Kunti and Madri as to how they could be mothers to illustrious children even though he himself was incapacitated to do so.

It is well within the precincts of laws of Nature to adopt a child from a willing parent or allow the lady to have a child from another man's semen. Sharadandayani, the wife of a warrior was instructed to have children by the elders of her family. Having a child through her husband was not possible. She left home in search of a learned man who would be willing to fill her womb. When she came across the accomplished one, she went and lived with him and became a mother to three brilliant sons.

Pandu requests Kunti to beget him a child in a similar fashion. Kunti refused to comply with Pandu's suggestion. She said she would never imagine uniting with another man but him.

There is a story about king Vyushitashava which Pandu recounts. Vyushitashava with his strength conquered the whole earth till the boundaries of the oceans. He protected all his subjects like his own children. He had plentiful of soma extracted, an elixir of life, and performed the Somasanstha sacrifice. In spite of living such an accomplished life the king died young.

Vyushitashava had a beautiful wife Bhadra. He loved her immensely. Both had intense desire for each other. But the king died of consumption leaving Bhadra weeping in misery and helplessness. She had no children to fill the vacuum created. She wailed in agony next to the king's corpse. Their love was immense; Bhadra felt as though the king was commanding her to continue his lineage. With the memories of her husband in her heart, she gave birth to three Shalvas and four Madras.

Pandu went on further to explain Dharma as laid out for women by Brahma. At the beginning of civilization women moved around freely. They spent time with anyone they fancied. There were no limitations. But at times this freewheeling lifestyle had serious repercussions.

Maharshi Uddalaka had a son Shvetaketu. Shvetaketu was a great scholar himself. Once he came across a rishi who forcibly tried to take his mother away. This angered the son to no end. The father tried to pacify the son. He explained that it was within the precincts of law to willingly or forcibly take away any woman one fancied. The furious Shvetaketu refused to accept this inhuman treatment. He issued a decree that once married a woman would remain faithful all her life to her husband and not associate with any other man for sexual relationship. If so it would be a sin. A man in turn would never try to seduce another man's wife or a virgin. Once married it was a woman's duty to bear children for the welfare of Universe, and refusal to do so would be a sin.

Great warriors for medical reasons if unable to give progenies to Brahma requested their wives to go to illustrious ascetics and beget children. Pandu was born to Krishna Dvaipyana after the death of his father, likewise he requested his wife Kunti to beget a child since he himself was unable to procreate but craved for a progeny.

On hearing Pandu's, account, Kunti recounted the words of rishi Durvasa who had blessed her with illustrious offsprings when she was a maiden. To fulfil her husband's desire she united with an illustrious sage. Kunti became a mother to a very famous son. He was named Yudhishthira. Right from birth the boy was righteous and honest.

Pandu being a warrior at heart now wished to have more children. Kunti as per her husband's desire became a mother to a very strong son. He was said to have enough strength to move mountains. Pandu named him Bhim. People lovingly called him Vayu putra. On the day of Bhim's birth, Duryodhan too was born.

Next as per her prayers Kunti was blessed with a son as powerful as lord Indra, the rain god. He came on this earth as the saviour of law abiding relations and worked for their welfare. He would annihilate all enemies of mankind. Thus Arjun came to the world.

Unfortunately human nature is never satisfied with just enough of goodness. It craves for more and more. Nature had blessed Pandu with three gems. But he longed to have more. Kunti reprimanded him. She felt it would be covetousness to keep wishing for more and not be thankful to Brahma for the gifts he had given. Greed was driving Pandu insane. He had lost his sense of reasoning.

In the meantime, Madri was getting restless and envious. Kunti was the mother to three radiant children. Dhritharashtra's wife too was a mother. It was she alone whose cradle was wanting of children. Out of desperation she approached Pandu and expressed her desire.

Pandu was overjoyed at the suggestion. He had a strong desire to increase his brood. He instructed Kunti to help Madri find a valorous sage who would bring spring to the queen's deserted womb. Madri united with a brilliant soul. She gave birth to twin sons. Brahma blessed them whole heartedly. The first son was named Nakula and the second Sahdeva. Pandu's sons were called Pandavs.

PANDU IS NO MORE

Pandu was yet not content. He requested Kunti to help Madri give him one more child. But Kunti now felt threatened. With the birth of one more child Madri's status would be equal to hers. In all humbleness she excused herself from the job. Pandu had no choice but to be content. Pandu had the pleasure of seeing his radiant handsome sons grow in the beautiful forests of Shatashringa mountains. The boys and their mothers had the protection of Pandu's presence. The young ones exhibited all signs of being valorous warriors. They were trained to be powerful archers. The king too lived languidly in the forest with his wives and children.

Till now Pandu had had his sensual desires under control since the death of sage Kindama. The curse of the sage had haunted and disturbed the king to no end for very long. But time heals all. With the birth of his sons, his inclination towards domesticity again started taking wings.

He began to feel the feminine presence of his wife Madri around him. Madri sensed Pandu's growing attraction towards her. She had not forgotten anything. She on her part tried to ward off his advances. Desire had taken control off Pandu's senses. The heart began to control the mind. Once in solitude he tried to get close to Madri. She did everything to avoid any union between the two. The excitement proved too fatal for the aging monarch. His heart missed the beats. He ended up lifeless in his wife's arms. Madri was too stunned to react.

Once she came out of her stupor she called out for Kunti. It did not take Kunti much time to assuage the situation. In desperation she accused Madri of being irresponsible and seducing the king. But death is destiny. The Brahmin's curse was imminent. This was poetic justice.

Very gracefully Madri took the onus of the entire incident on herself. She told Kunti that she could not resist the charms of the Puru king and was tempted. Kunti countered by adding that Madri had the love of the monarch which he had restrained towards her but being the eldest of the two wives it was her privilege to end her life along with her husband's on the funeral pyre.

Madri held herself responsible for Pandu's death. She requested Kunti to take care of her sons as her own and sought permission to leave the world along with her husband. Madri sat on her husband's funeral pyre to end her journey of life.

PANDAVS RETURN TO HASTINAPUR

The ascetics at mount Shatashringa who were Pandu's companions performed the last rites. It was the collective opinion of one and all that the boys and their mother would be best protected in their home town of Hastinapur and not in the rough terrains of a mountain that too without a father.

A journey of battles with hardships and integrity began for Kunti and her sons. They all trudged back home, reaching the gates of Hastinapur. The dwellers were baffled to see so the sons of Pandu who had left the throne long ago. People came out of their houses. Baffled Bhishma, Dhritarashtra, Vidhura, Satyavati and Gandhari reached the royal gate. Dhritrashtra's sons dressed in all their finery too reached.

The most revered of the fellow travelers who had accompanied the Pandavs introduced them to their elders. Pandu was not their biological father. They all had came to this world through surrogates hence were called children of God; Yudhisthira the righteous was known as Dharma Putra. Bhim was called Vayuputra. Arjun the invincible warrior was called Indra's son and the twins Nakul and Sahdev as Sun gods, Ashvins.

Pandu took keen interest in the welfare and education of his children. The boys were groomed in the art of warfare and in the studies of Philosphy.

Royal funeral rites were performed for Pandu and Madri. All the hermits who had accompanied them left for the forest. Lots of riches were given away as alms to the poor. Bhishma, Vidhura and Pandu's sons wept in agony. Later homage ceremony was performed for Pandu. The cake of immortality was distributed. The citizens of Hastinapur lamented the death of their monarch. The city was immersed in grief. The whole city along with the sons grieved for twelve nights.

Krishna Dvaipayna too came to pay homage to the departed soul of his biological son. He prophesied the beginning of an era of evil. He talked to his mother Satyavati and told her that there would be a decline in human value system. People would have little respect for

Justice. There would be lots of conniving and delusions. It would be best for her to denounce the life of domesticity and live in a hermitage.

Satyavati had lots of respect for Vyasa's vision. She urged her daughter in laws Koushalya and Ambalika to also join her as the illustrious Bharata lineage would be taking its last breath in no time; thanks to the evil deeds of its descendants. All the three ladies left for the forest living the life of ascetics and giving up the perishable body for onwards journey.

The Pandavs started their life in their father's house. They would play with their uncle Dhritrashtra's sons. But having lived a hard and disciplined life in the forest they excelled in every field.

Bhimsena the strongest of the lot would bully his cousins playfully. With his great energy he would beat them to pulp. With the passage of time resentment started building up against the Pandavs. But Bhimsena bore no ill will towards his cousins since he was only a child. But a storm started brewing in Dhritrashtra's abode. His eldest and most powerful son Duryodhan was driven insane by the fame of Bhimsena's strength. He started devising means and ways of eliminating him from his path. He had lost his sense of reasoning.

PRECEPTOR OF KURUS; DRONA

Sharadvat was skilled in the study of warfare. His father saw in him all the qualities of an inborn warrior. Sharadvat gained the knowledge through lots of penance and hard work. With a bow and arrow always in his hand he hardly looked at the women around him. Unknown to him the beautiful Janapadi engaged in every possible effort to attract his attention. Sharadvat succumbed to the lady's charms. Twins were born to him. From birth only the children were looked after by the forest dwellers.

Once Shantanu beheld the twins in deer skin with bows and arrows slung on their sides, in the forest. From his deep insight he knew that they were from the Brahmin lineage and would be great warriors in future. Out of compassion he took them back home. He treated the both as his own. They were named Kripa and Kripi.

In the meantime Sharadvat had become an expert in the knowledge of warfare. When he learnt of Kripa and Kripi he knew they were his own children. Without any reservation he disclosed the secret of their lineage. Kripa trained under his father Sharadvat.

The Pandavs and their cousins too trained under Sharadvat. When the training was complete, Bhishma set out looking for a new preceptor who was illustrious, disciplined and adept in archery. Drona was the best candidate. He had intense knowledge of weapons of mass destruction namely the Agni weapons that charred the opponent to ashes.

Draupada and Drona had played together in the latter's hermitage as children. Draupada's father king Prishata and Drona's father the great sage Bharadvaja were friends too. After the death of his father Prishata Drapuda ascended the throne. He was now the king of northern Panchala.

In the meantime Drona married Kripi, daughter of Sharadvat. He had a valorous son Ashvathamma who was said to have the strength of a horse. Drona spent all his time learning the art of warfare and imparting it to his son and Kshatriya students. He sought the patronage of his influential friends and acquaintances for survival.

The Kshatriya Brahmin Parasurama before leaving for the forest gave away all his weapons to Drona. But his childhood friend Drupada now a king treated him with disdain. He very subtly projected his superiority over the ascetic. This did not go down well with Drona. Seething with anger he returned without asking for anything vowing to seek revenge in future.

Draupada, had talked at length on the philosophy of equality. Equality based on the principle of wealth, status and lineage. To him friendship was nothing but a matter of necessity. Once the purpose was fulfilled, friendship died a natural death. Learned and wise that he was, Drona thought it essential to instil some sense in the otherwise inflated Draupada and settle scores with him.

From Panchala he went straight to Hastinapur. One fine day on beholding the Kuru princes sporting in the forest, he set out to test their skills both physical and mental. A ball fell in the well. After struggling for long the boys were unable to retrieve. Drona made a chain with arrows and piercing the ball with one end and pulled it out. Everyone present was dumbstruck with his skill and intelligence. They went back and told Bhishma of the feat.

Bhishma realised that his search for a preceptor had come to an end. He had found a skilful teacher for his grandsons. In all earnestness he put forth his request before Drona. The rishi too opened up. He told Bhishma of his visit to Panchala king, Draupada. Both of them had learnt Dhanur veda under maharshi Agniveshya. They were friends and Draupada had promised to extend financial patronage once he ascended the throne. When time came he had mocked Drona"s inferior financial status and social viability compared to his. To add insult to injury he had haughtily declared that just like the fool and learned could not be friends so could the rich and poor. Drona, now wanted great kshatriya students who in future would fight on his behalf and bring Draupad to dust

Along with abundant riches Bhishma sent Kuru boys to be trained under Drona. Princes from other states too joined in, like the Vrishnis, the Andhalakas including Karna. Karna and Arjuna competed.

Duryodhan tried to make the best of the situation arising out of enmity between two skillful warriors. Karna too found a sympathiser in Duryodhan in the otherwise cruel world of the rich and mighty. Duryodhan the man from high lineage tries to exploit a man emotionally battered by the very cousins whom he loathes for their superior skills.

Of all of Drona's students Arjuna was closest to his heart. Arjuna's devotion towards both his preceptor and his teachings was incomprehensible. Arjuna would begin practising the moment the sun set. It seems his passion was such that if at all the sun got overshadowed by the clouds without a moment's thought he would pick his bow and arrow.

Arjun's diligence endeared him to Drona. He touched his preceptor's heart like no other student had managed to do. Drona in turn promised to help him reach pinnacles of success which no one had tread before. He wholeheartedly gave all he had to his student.

THE RISE AND FALL OF EKLAVYA

The princes learnt the use of bow and arrow while on an elephant, horseback, chariots and from the ground. Not only archery Drona taught his disciples to fight with clubs, swords, spears, javelins and lances. Princes from all other states too learnt Dhanur veda from Drona. But Eklavya, son of tribal king Hiranyadhanu was denied a place. Eklavya's so called low parentage, birth from the union of a Brahmin and a Shudra came in the way.

Drona did not wish to incur the wrath of Kshatriya clan. He wanted to maintain friendly relations with the kshatriyas to humble Draupada. But the feisty boy did not let this discourage him from following his passion. He practised hard in the presence of Drona's mud statue every day. Entirely owing to his own zeal he learnt the fine art of archery.

Once Pandavs and Dhrithrashtra's sons the Kauravs along with their dog went to the forest. Eklavya who at that time was practising blindfolded got distracted by the barking. He filled the dog's mouth with arrows to shut the menace. The princes were amazed. They went out in search of the archer. On encountering the lowly forest dweller they were filled with envy.

He was likely to give them a tough competition in future. Like spoilt children who would not share their parent's affection with anyone else they went up to Drona and complained. The indulgent preceptor called upon Eklavya and asked for his tutoring charges since he was the source of inspiration.

The boy so deep into hero worship readily obliged. Without any remorse or anger he gave away his right thumb. His mind was at peace and so was Arjuna's. Arjuna had managed to eliminate competition but earned the wrath of Almighty Universe for his act of insolence. Without the thumb the swiftness in shooting was gone.

Drona's prophecy came true. There was no longer an archer more skilful than Arjuna. Duryodhan and Bhim mastered the clubs. The twins' Sahdev and Nakula excelled in sword fighting. Ashvathamma, Drona's son gained knowledge of weapons of mass destruction.

Once Drona came in close contact with a crocodile in a river. Just to test his students' skills he frantically called for help. While others gaped Arjun simply sliced the beast to pieces. Drona, immensely pleased bestowed on him the Brahmashira, a weapon of mass destruction. He advised him to never use it on the weak but on someone stronger than him. Brahmashira when used would char a city to ashes. So lots of prudence was required. The preceptor blessed his disciple with invincibility.

Unfortunately Arjun's fame and skill invoked envy and hatred in Duryodhan. Arjuna was an exceptional student who was extremely focussed. But this pleased Drona to no end. He had found a weapon that would avenge his humiliation at the hands of Draupad. Mission accomplished.

CHAPTER EIGHT
Jatugriha Daha Parva

The Kuru princes had completed their education with Drona. At the end of the term Drona approached Bhishma and expressed his desire to let his students exhibit all that they had learnt in the presence of the entire town.

His proposal was well accepted. Dhritrashtra felt defeated. He wished to see the royal spectacle with his own eyes. He instructed Vidhur to make all the arrangements. A large stretch of land was cleared and flattened. It was equipped with various types of weapons.

On the anointed day Dhritrashtra arrived accompanied by Bhishma and his advisors. Gandhari and Kunti too came to witness the royal spectacle. The whole town gathered. Drona dressed in white garments, radiant as the moon and accompanied by his son Ashvathamma arrived.

Brahmins recited verses to mark the beginning of the auspicious event. Brave warriors of the Bharata dynasty were being led by Yudhisthira. They carried bows, quivers and wore finger protectors. In order of their ages they displayed their skills. The spectators gaped in wonder and amazement.

Bhimsena and Duryodhan displayed the use of clubs. Both of them appeared like hungry lions trying to corner the other. Vidhur was the eyes to Dhritrashtra and Kunti to Gandhari. The crowd was divided over the two. Some cheered for Duryodhan while others for Bhim.

Drona himself announced the arrival of his favourite protégée Arjuna. His voice reflected pride. The audience were in awe of the hero. Kunti was a happy mother. Loud noises of cheering crowd reached Dhritrashtra's ears. He felt elated that his kingdom would have the privilege of having a warrior of Arjun's stature.

Arjun exhibited the use of weapons to the entire assembly present. His movements were lithe and agile. He exhibited his skills in shooting.

Drona stood surrounded by the Pandavas. A jealous Duryodhan, his vicious friend Ashvathamma and his numerous brothers too were present They together looked like demons out to attack goodness.

ENTERS HALF-BROTHER KARNA

Next to enter was the mighty Karna. He was born to Kunti when she was still a virgin. He was clad in humble minimal clothes with an armour. The young man epitomised strength. He appeared radiant and handsome. Before starting to exhibit his feat he bowed in obeisance to Drona and Kripa.

People present wished to be introduced to the warrior who appeared like a tiger. Very confidently the youth replied that in no time he would exhibit feats that would make Arjun's appear pale in comparison. He proved true to his word. The spectators gaped in amazement. The boy had auspicious marks on his body that showed he was a born warrior. Duryodhan and his brothers felt a strange kinship with the unknown stranger who had outshone their brilliant cousins.

Arjun was envious. An outsider had come and taken the winds off his sails. Duryodhan wasted no time in trying to befriend him. All the brothers congratulated him wholeheartedly. They expressed immense appreciation at the display of his skill; which was equal to their cousin Arjun's.

Karna thanked Duryodhan for his friendship and support. He wished to duel Arjun in future seeking Duryodhan's approval and patronage. Arjun felt insulted and intimidated. He vowed to eliminate the competitor, for the battle ground was exclusively for kings and princes and not outsiders. Karna who was highly skilled was not nervous at the prospect. Rather he reprimanded him for wasting time on glib talk and not using his arrows to settle scores. It is only the weak who talk and do nothing. Cheered by their respective warring sides, both the high calibre warriors stood facing each other, wanting to eliminate the other. The mighty Rain showered its blessings.

Ashvathamma, Duryodhan and his brothers had all their hopes centred on Karna. Kripa, Drona and the Pandavas were proud of Arjun. But Kunti's mind was in turmoil. One look at Karna and the birth marks on his body and she immediately knew he was her own son. Both her sons stood against each other, clad in armour. Destiny had played a cruel trick. She passed out in grief.

Both the warriors took their respective positions and held their bows high to start. Sharadvat Kripa introduced Arjun as the son of Kunti and Pandu of the illustrious Kuru lineage to the assembly of people present. He then asked Karna to introduce himself. It was permissible for warriors of same status to duel and not otherwise. Princes would fight with princes alone that too of royal lineage. Blood appeared to drain out of Karna's countenance. He was speechless. His skill and lineage were at crossroads. One he had inherited without any choice and the other he had acquired with lots of hard work and penance.

Duryodhan sensed his predicament. He did not wish to lose the opportunity of using Karna against his skilful cousins. Without wasting time and rising to the moment he declared that he would instate Karna on the throne of Anga with full honour. Karna would be a king in his own right and no circumstances would prevent him from fighting the Pandavas. Karna felt extremely humbled by Duryodhana's show of love and affection who was the prince of Hastinapur.

Karna wished to pay back the debt. Duryodhan once again played his cards. He made a place for himself in Karna's life by asking for nothing in turn but his eternal and unquestioning friendship. Fate had again tricked Karna. Duryodhan was using him against his own righteous cousins to satisfy his unholy ends.

Karna's father Adhiratha on hearing the commotion and activity in the city came in to witness the scenario. He had heard that his son Karna had been coronated as the king of Anga. The proud emotional father hugged his son. But on witnessing the assembly of kings and princes excitement gave way to embarrassment. He felt conscious of his inferior stature and attire.

On the other hand Arjun had started feeling insecure. Karna would prove to be a tough adversary in future. Moreover Duryodhan was using him as a weapon. The brothers wanted him out of the equation. In desperation Bhim made fun of Karna's parentage. He was the son of a charioteer. It would be befitting for him to have a whip rather than a bow in his hand, he jeered. A crown would look appropriate on kings and princes and not on charioteers, he teased adding insult to injury. Karna just stood rooted and humiliated at the barbed comments hurled at him.

Duryodhan sensed his game plan failing. After the sparks that flew from Bhim, Karna would possibly refuse to accept the lordship of

Anga and not fight at all in the battle field. He immediately came forward and put up a strong defence in favour of Karna.

Duryodhan reprimanded Bhim for taking pot shots at Karna's lineage which was irrelevant in a battle field. The only virtue a warrior needed to have was strength and skill. Every warrior irrespective of his lineage needed a fair chance to fight and prove himself. Just like the source of fire was water, the birth of a skilful warrior did not have to be from a warrior. Ascetics have been known to give birth to brave warriors. Similarly weapons used to kill demons was made by the skillful ascetic Dadhichi. Parentage of rishi Guha till date was a mere speculation. Karna appeared to be the son of a great warrior, from the marks he had on his body. Finally Duryodhan challenged his cousins to mount Karna's chariot, and break his bow if at all they wanted him out of the equation. Putting an end to all speculations Duryodhan restored Karna's faith in him.

The loyalties of the crowd present were divided. Some were in for Arjun, others for Duryodhan and quite a few for Karna. Kunti was happy for her son. He was now the king of Anga.

Duryodhan on the other hand was delighted. He now had a strong weapon in the form of Karna. He was now no longer afraid of his cousins. He would fight them tooth and nail. Karna in his highly charged emotional state thanked Duryodhan who had defended and stood by him. His humiliation had been avenged. He was now a king and was no longer the low strata charioteer's son.

DRONA'S REVENGE ON DRAUPADA

With his pupil now highly skilled in warfare Drona assigned them the task of bringing to dust his friend turned foe Draupada. All the boys mounted their chariots and marched up to the city of Panchala, well equipped with their weapons. They destroyed the entire city and captured the powerful Draupada along with his advisors.

Humiliated, humbled and robbed of wealth and kingdom Draupada was made to appear before Drona. With vengeance in heart Drona very succinctly offered to be his friend. He sarcastically wished to know whether he would like to maintain a relationship since economically and stature wise both were equal. He further added that he would like to retain half of his kingdom since Draupada would not want to be friends with a man who was not a king.

Accordingly he gave away the insignificant southern part of Panchala known as Makandi to Draupada and kept the major northern part Ahichhatra with himself. He set him free saying that he was an ascetic and not a warrior who would take other people's lives. Physically Draupada had been set free but emotionally he was seething, knotted up, humiliated, and enslaved to Drona.

Losing his kingdom and self respect to Drona made Draupada restless and agitated. He felt defeated. Drona's powers both as a warrior and a scholar were greater to his and there was no way they could be surpassed. He prayed for the birth of a son who would avenge his humiliation.

THE GAME BEGINS

The Pandava brothers had become extremely strong and powerful. In spite of Karna's skill and support Duryodhana's insecurities refused to die down. Adding fuel to fire, the people of Hastinapur too started talking about their valour and good conduct. They felt that the oldest, Yudhisthira, would make an excellent king. He was wise, righteous, compassionate and learned. It was high time he be crowned.

From his demeanour it was likely that he would have lots of respect for Bhishma, Vidura, Dhritrashtra and their progenies who would never be in want of sustenance. Such whispers burnt a hole in Duryodhan's heart. He was engulfed in anger and envy.

Duryodhan marched up to his father and twisted the entire narrative. He told him that even though he had all the qualities of a king apparent; he was denied the right owing to his blindness for no fault of his. Pandu was instated as the king. Now his son would inherit the throne lawfully. And moreover Yudhisthira was the eldest of the lot. So it would have to be him ultimately. Above all, Yudhisthira had the approval and love of the elders and the people of Hastinapur. But had Dhritrashtra been the king his sons would inherit the throne and the generations to come.

But destiny had played a cruel trick. People of Hastinapur wanted Yudhisthira to be the king. Duryodhan was upset over the fact that their entire generation would have to be subservient to the Pandavas and would never be kings. With a conniving mind Duryodhan wished to go to any length to snatch the kingdom from his cousins.

Dhritarashtra was wise, old and evil. He explained his viewpoint to his son. He felt his brother Pandu, who was good and honest was loved immensely by his people. Pandu, had a great relationship with his allies, advisors, soldiers and was a benevolent benefactor even to their children and grandchildren.

He had earned the good will of his people and their future generations. Dhritrashtra was afraid that all those citizens would accept no one else but Yudhisthira on the throne. But his equally devious son had a solution to every problem. The reigns of the kingdom were in Dhrithrashtra's hands temporarily since Pandu's death. He could influence the people and advisors with gifts and honour.

Duryodhan wished to send away the five brothers and their mother to another town. In the meantime he would be coronated as the king. But again there was a hitch which the father thought could cause impediment in their plans. Vidhur, Drona, Kripa and Bhishma would not approve of it. The wise never favour differences but instead stood against them.

Duryodhan had thought about that beforehand. Drona's son Ashvathamma was his friend. It was obvious that both the father son duo would be on his side even though Drona was very fond of the Pandavs especially Arjun. Sharadvat Kripa was Asvathamma's maternal uncle and would never abandon him. Bhishma's approach would be one of righteousness and not of prejudice and bias. Vidura had deep love and affection for Pandavs but his loyalties were always with the kingdom of Hastinapur and would never abandon it.

Having ruled out all opposition, Duryodhan ordered his father to send the Pandavs away and complete the mission in their absence. Both set out to execute their evil plan. Thus began the game. On Dhritrashtra's advice some advisors talked very highly of a place called Varanavata to tempt. This aroused curiosity and excitement. Dhritrashtra sensed this and as planned used the opportunity to suit his purpose. He asked all of them to migrate there. Yudhisthira found it difficult to turn down his uncle's command and moreover he had no allies to support him.

Along with his mother and brothers Yudhisthira set out for the journey. But the evil and conniving Duryodhan had more venom left. He approached his most trusted advisor Purochana. He tempted the equally evil one with lots of wealth and honour once he himself was the king. Purochana was assigned the task of eliminating the brothers in Varanavata without anyone's knowledge and suspicion. He was asked to build a house of inflammable material. Kunti and her sons along with their attendants would be made to live there. Task was initiated but not accomplished yet.

Bhishma, Vidura, Drona and Kripa were sad and unhappy at Dhritarashtra's decision; but did not say anything. The Pandavas would have to incur the wrath of his evil son Duryodhan. But some fearless Brahmins voiced their frank opinion; Dhritrashtra is a jealous partial man. Pandu's sons are very much like Pandu himself; strong, free from vice and abide by rules of righteousness. Since Pandu was the king, his sons are the true inheritors of the kingdom. But Dhritrashtra's evilness prevents him from giving them what is rightfully theirs. It is unfortunate that everything happened in Bhishma's presence. All the Brahmins wished to leave Hastinapur and move to the city of Varanavata.

Although sad and troubled, Yudhisthira never suspected his uncle's intentions. He felt he was a father figure and not to be doubted. He even requested the Brahmins to not do so. Eventually they were blessed wholeheartedly and wished well in future.

Vidhura warned the Pandavs. He imparted wisdom like a father would subtly in riddles lest it offended the others present. He told Yudhisthira that in the cruel world of men and vice only knowledge and insight would protect them all. A sharp object kills once but deceit kills without the victim being aware of the perpetrator. One better not play with fire, even be it sun's, for both burn. It is better to keep away from people who are likely to harm you. With knowledge and insight, try to sense danger and keep away from it. Even when there is no apparent danger around still it may not be safe. Use intelligence and try to perceive the invisible lurking in the background. Perseverance is man's biggest asset. A restless man is always in hurry and never achieves anything. One should always maintain distance from untrustworthy friends whose help is likely to cause damage. A person who has his five senses under control can never be oppressed by enemy. The elders blessed and wished them safety and happiness.

Yudhisthira alerted his brothers of the trials and tribulations they would face in future. He warned them to protect themselves from evil. Intelligence and insight would be their guiding principle. It would be better to visualize and understand the invisible rather than get carried away by what was apparent. The best way to escape from the clutches of a cunning man and from the burden of his worthless gratitude was by being hard and strong. There was always danger from evil intentions be it of human beings or animals. Both killed.

EXIT HASTINAPUR ENTERS VARANAVAT

The Pandavs were welcomed warmly by the people of Varanavata. They chanted victory in unison and paid obeisance. Purochana was there to receive them and escort them to their house. All their comforts were looked after with utmost sincerity. Purochana was always in attendance. But Yudhisthira was perturbed.

The newly built house smelt of lac and ghee. It was clear that it was made of inflammable material intended to burn the residents to death. Purochana was up to something. After winning the confidence of the boys he wished to eliminate them. Probably Vidhur had foreseen the turn of events and warned Yudhishtira. Purochana was acting on Duryodhan's behest.

Yudhisthira advised his brothers to not react but play along to fool the deceptor and beat him at his own game. Purochana and Duryodhan were both unscrupulous. They would not mind stooping low to satisfy their ends. If one plot got foiled they would have another up their sleeve until they had accomplished their mission.

Duryodhan had powerful allies, large treasury and clout, whereas Pandu's sons had none except the goodwill of their people. The best option was to deceive both into thinking that their master plan had worked and the brothers were dead in the fire. Instead the Pandavs would burn down the house themselves, escape and move into a life of anonymity, wandering from one place to another lest be tracked and killed. A secret tunnel dug from the house was the best escape route.

Vidura was an intelligent man. Though he never exerted authority he was a benign presence in the royal household. He had heard of a conspiracy wherein Duryodhan planned to eliminate the Pandavas. He immediately dispatched an extremely trusted mason to built a tunnel, an escape route from the house.

It was amply clear that the inflammable house was built at the behest of evil Duryodhan. He would leave no stone unturned to deprive his cousins of their rightful share and place in the kingdom. Vidhur with his vision and foresight was well aware of that. Both the tunnel digger and the boys worked in tandem to deceive Purochana.

A tunnel was being dug extremely stealthily and in the meantime the Pandavs spent their days hunting in the forests putting on a facade of contentment and trust. No one was aware of the storm brewing within. The house was sitting on a time bomb. It had a huge armoury in the basement waiting to be ignited. Purochana on the other hand was delighted that he had managed to win trust.

The tunnel was ready. A day before escaping Kunti offered food to Brahmins seeking their blessings. Lots of villagers too came for the feast. In the darkness of night Pandavs and Kunti set out towards their journey of anonymity. To give final touches to the mission Bhim torched the armoury. There were a series of loud blasts. The villagers came running from their homes in the middle of night, hearing the commotion. The house was in flames. The villagers cursed Duryodhan, Dhritrashtra, and their ally Purochana. Purochana had fallen in the grave he had dug.

The boys along with their mother had managed to escape. Bhima was the greatest source of strength. He would carry his mother on his back when she was too tired to walk.

People of Hastinapur were angry with Vidhur and Bhishma too for being unable to rein the evil Duryodhan.

The news made Dhritrashtra both happy and sad. His younger brother had died in the true sense. His lineage had come to an end. But he was content with the knowledge that his own lineage would have kings, the honour he himself was denied for no fault of his. In the atmosphere of sorrow Vidura did not grieve much. He was aware of the truth.

The Pandavs after their escape from the ill fated house went through trying times. Hungry, tired and sleepless, with their fragile mother in tow they moved through the forest towards south, guided by the stars.

They dreaded the thought of being recognised and hunted by their evil cousin. Bhimsen led the way clearing the obstacles and carrying his mother when she would not walk out of tiredness.

The boys were distressed at seeing their mother in that plight. She had led a life of a princess at her father Kuntibhoja's house, was sister of the illustrious Vasudev, had been a mother to valorous sons and was queen of the famous Bharata lineage.

They were unhappy at seeing each other's state; each had seen the other radiant, valorous and full of honour. One black sheep in the family is enough to ruin the entire lineage.

CHAPTER NINE

Hidimba Vadha Parva

The Pandavs had initiated themselves into a life of anonymity. The path was dangerous. Forests, full of wilderness and danger lurking in every corner greeted them. But it never frightened the brave ones. No danger was too big for them. There was no evil they could not encounter. Once after long hours of trekking in the forest and hills all of them slept except for Bhima who kept guard.

Unfortunately to add to the struggles and hardships a man eating demon Hidimba cast his covetous eyes on them. Hidimba ordered his sister to go and kill the men in their sleep so that later both of them would devour their flesh in peace and enjoy. Following orders the sister set out to do as instructed by her brother. But unfortunately for her, Bhim was awake keeping guard.

Destiny had her own plans. Hidimba was smitten by the muscular, strong and powerful Bhim. She forgot her mission and had eyes only for him. She wished to be his beloved. Killing and devouring would gratify the senses only temporarily. But a husband's love would be perennial and ethereal. Putting on an act of demureness she warned Bhim of the impending dangers posed by her brother as it was his abode.

She wished to know the identity of Bhim's brothers who were fast asleep. Insane in love for Bhim she revealed that she had been sent by her brother who wished to see them all dead. She professed her love for the handsome Pandav and expressed her wish to marry him. Her infatuation was so intense that she even decided to abandon her brother and take Bhim in her wing and protect him from her brother's ire.

But Bhim refused to abandon his family for self gratification and safety. It would bring him no pleasure to see his loved ones as Hidimba's food. The demoness left no stone unturned to appease him. She even agreed to take his family along and protect them. Bhim was unmoved. He was strong enough to protect them all without her help from the demon's ire.

In the meantime the brother too came where Bhim and his sister were discussing matters. She had taken unusually long to complete the mission. He wished to see as to what was stopping her. His appearance was very much in synchronisation with his ways of life. He was huge, ugly and frightful. The sister on seeing her brother approach quietly asked Bhim to accompany her, along with his family to a safe place. She was aware of all the escape routes. Bhim felt insulted.

The demoness had underestimated him. He very calmly refused to comply and prepared himself for a duel with her brother. Bhim was a strong man. His movements were lithe like that of a tiger and had the strength of an elephant. The man eating forest dweller would find a tough adversary in him. Hidimba was furious at seeing his sister besotted, mad with desire and no longer afraid of his anger and venom.

She had changed sides. She had betrayed him and the community for wantonness, he seethed. She was no longer the sister he loved but an enemy who along with the Pandavas had to be done away with. He wished to take her life before he took theirs.

In a fit of fury he lugged at her wanting to strangulate. Bhim stood in the way counterfeiting the attack. Hidimba stood immobilised even more furious experiencing the strength of the youth. Bhimsena mocked him. "Do not fight your sister for she has done no wrong. She followed your instructions but was filled with desire at the sight of my youth. Her heart and mind are no longer in control. Moreover I shall never allow a woman to be killed in my presence. Leave her alone and fight me, he jeered. All the inhabitants of the forest would welcome the news of your death with a sigh of relief. They would be able to move about fearlessly and live in peace. Justice shall prevail".

Hidimba was losing patience. He challenged Bhim to a duel and asked him to stop preaching. He professed he was stronger than him and set the rules for the fight. He vowed to first eliminate Bhim and then deal with his family and sister. The great fight began between the two. Each knocked the other down tearing, dragging and clawing Both had immense strength and energy.

In the meantime the other brothers and Kunti too got up from their sleep. Kunti was struck by the beauty and comeliness of the demon girl. Hidimba did not hide the fact that she was the man eater's sister and that her primary intentions had been not too noble.

Bhim and her brother were fighting a little distance away. Unfortunately Bhim appeared to be a little overwhelmed and cowed down. To boost his confidence Yudhisthra very slyly offered to help. Bhim's self respect and ego took a beating. He asked his brother to quietly sit and watch the spectacle. The fight had to come to an end soon for possibly Hidimba would start using deception to win.

Bhim was enraged at the giant's viciousness and ways of life. He had led an unholy existence, giving pain to others and rejoicing in their sufferings. This needed to stop. Arjun goaded Bhim to act swiftly and put an end to his miserable existence. Joyous at the end of evil, all of them along with Hidimba's sister left for another destination lest be discovered by Duryodhan.

Bhim was afraid that in spite of the demonesse's claims of love and devotion, she was likely to use deception to kill his entire family. He had killed her brother. Out of revenge and in continuation with her demonic ways of life she was bound to be her old self. Accordingly he wished to send her where her brother had reached.

But Yudhisthira advised him against doing so. It was unethical to kill a woman. Moreover if Bhim could over power her immensely powerful brother and doing the same to the lady would be no problem. Love struck Hidimba on the other hand was on an entirely different plane. She had betrayed her own brother, family and community for her passion and desire for Bhim. There was no other place where she would go.

BIRTH OF GHATOTKACHA

Hidimba requested Kunti to permit and convince her son to marry her. Kunti felt morally obligated since she had been faithful to her entire family and even saved them. On the other hand Hidimba was sure to die of remorse if at all rejected.

Seeking Kunti's blessings Hidimba co joined with Bhim in holy matrimony. She set up home and hearth, in another forest away from his family. But the Pandav came to meet them every night as he had promised his mother. Hidimba assumed the avatar of a wise and comely lady.

As a good wife she would indulge in pleasure with the Pandav. Very shortly they became parents to a very strong, huge, dark and energetic son. He was shiny and round like a pot, likewise named Ghatotkacha.

He was one with the Pandavs. But time stops for none. They had to move on to another unknown destination.

Hidimba and her son Ghatotkacha stayed back. The forest was her abode. She would not be able to adapt elsewhere. Moreover the future course of life for Bhim and his brothers was quite uncertain. Hidimba along with her son promised to come whenever called for. The birth of the boy was not without purpose. He had been created by Brahma to be great soul Karna's nemesis. With a heavy heart all parted and took leave.

The brothers along with their mother travelled extensively through the forests. They would slow down when the imminent danger was apparently less. Their hair had grown long and matted. Old clothes were now replaced by deer skin. In transition while camping, they would under the guidance of ascetics study philosophy and the art of warfare.

On their way they came across their grandfather VedaVyas. All paid obeisance to the aging rishi. The old man was full of love for the young boys. He loved all his grandchildren equally but the wronged youngsters touched his heart.

Vyasa confessed that he had a premonition of things to come. He had an inherent feel that Dhritrashtra would not give them their rightful place and share in the kingdom. But it was not a matter of sorrow. For adversity brings out the best in human beings. Happiness shall follow. He advised them to go to the nearby town of Ekachakra and live there in disguise as it was safe. He promised to come and instruct them for the further course of action.

Ved Vyasa blessed Kunti. He asked her to banish all fear and insecurities. She had been blessed with sagacious sons. Yudhisthira would rule the earth aided by his strong brothers' Bhim and Arjun. Madri's sons

Nakula and Sahdev would be their constant companions. They would be kings and give away alms to the poor and offer patronage to the ascetics. Moreover happiness befriends those who learn to adapt with place and time.

CHAPTER TEN

Baka Vadha Parva

TOWN OF EKACHAKRA

Yudhisthira along with Kunti and his brothers moved to the town of Ekachakra. A poor Brahmin who lived with his family offered them a place to stay in the outer part of the house. Thus began a new phase in their life. Kunti would stay back while the brothers spent the days begging for alms. By evening all of them would be home.

They would give everything they got to their mother who would divide it equally amongst the brothers with Bhim getting a bigger share in the food. The kshatriyas lived safely in the house of the Brahmin away from the clutches of evil Duryodhan. The guests were respected and treated well. All of them lived in peace. One fine day when the boys had left except for Bhim, Kunti heard loud wailing and sounds of distress coming from the Brahmin's quarters. Kunti got alarmed and disturbed by the commotion.

She wished to go and help. It was time for them to pay back. A good righteous one returns more than what he receives! She and her sons would help them, no matter how grave the situation.

The family appeared to be grief stricken. The Brahmin lived in the house bestowed on his wife by her father. Although all her relations were no longer alive the lady did not wish to leave the place. The Brahmin reprimanded his wife. Her desire for worldly possessions had landed the entire family in grave trouble wherein they would have to lose one member of the family.

THE DEMON; BAKA

In his distressed state of mind the Brahmin was in an introspective mood. For him life on earth was full of suffering and misery. To keep body and soul together, one has to follow the path of righteousness, create wealth and have children to carry on the lineage. All the three forces are contradictory in character and pursuing those lead to misery. There is no redemption from the sins we commit. To survive we need wealth. But how much is enough is extremely abstract. In our desire for acquiring wealth we lose peace of mind which makes us miserable. Losing acquired riches adds to the catastrophe. Attachment to acquisitions torments the soul like a master torments the slave.

The Brahmin was faced with the dilemma of losing one of his family members. It was tearing his heart apart. The situation had arisen because of the wife's love for the dead relations and their possessions. The Brahmin's mind was in turmoil.

His wife had been a constant companion. In distress she had been a mother, a friend. She came from a noble family and was chosen for him by his parents. Both of them had been married in accordance with law and with the approval of elders. She had been a good mother and a faithful wife.

The very thought of losing his daughter made him even more miserable. She had been a god's gift to him. It was his duty to protect her in turn. He had loved his children both, son and daughter, equally.

Once married, his daughter's children would ensure continuity of his lineage. The thought of sacrificing himself instead of his family tormented the Brahmin even more.

The Brahmin's helplessness burnt a hole in his wife's heart. Death is destiny, so why grieve, she reprimanded. She felt it would be appropriate if she sacrificed her life for the welfare of her family. As a wife she had performed her duty of being a mother to two children. A father was more capable of supporting and protecting his children even without the help of his wife but it may not be possible for a mother to do so. Without the protection of a father or a husband, it is not possible for a woman to protect herself. Without the guidance of a father, the boy may not turn out to be as virtuous and learned. The daughter may not be able to maintain her innocence. Circumstances may force the woman to leave the path of virtue, the Brahmin's wife lamented. Without her husband's protective umbrella she shall be at the mercy of others who were bound to take advantage of her state. The entire family shall perish.

The lady sought her husband's permission. She wished to go on the last journey before he did and not live under the care of her sons. This was in accordance with Dharma. This was the path to salvation. Friends, children, wife and all the relations one nurtures come to rescue in times of distress.

And moreover the demon would never kill a woman for this was against dharma, which even they followed. She had no regrets. She had led a happy life. Her sacrifice would save her children, her husband and their lineage.

The daughter overheard her parents piteous and overwhelming cry of helplessness. She just could not see them in agony. She went up to them and sought permission to go to the demon. One day she would have to leave home, she argued. So it was appropriate that she left now. If at all her father or mother became the victim of the demon's outrage the whole family shall perish. She wished to sacrifice her life for the good of her family. Moreover it would be tormenting for the father to leave the family rudderless and begging for food.

Kunti was moved to tears. She wished to know the cause of their suffering and offered help. The Brahmin was of the opinion that it was beyond human realm to banish misery. But out of courtesy he narrated his woes. The town was under the control of a vicious and powerful man Baka. He protected the people from enemies and outside attacks. But in turn the residents had a heavy price to pay.

Every week one of the villagers had to supply Baka with a cart full of grains and one member of his family to be in his service for life. There was just no way out of the misery. If at all anyone tried to escape they were rounded and killed. The king Vetrakiyagriha was weak and imbecile. He made no effort to free his subjects from the terror unleashed by Baka.

Brahmins have the choice to choose the place they wish to live. It is always advisable to live in a place where the king is strong and benevolent, then start a family and finally acquire wealth. But out of avarice, the Brahmin's wife chose to stay back because of the house she had inherited. Her greed for riches had landed him in trouble wherein he would have to lose one of his family members. He wished to go to the demon with his entire family so that no one was left behind to mourn.

Kunti intervened beholding the entire family miserable. She offered to send her valorous son Bhim to the demon with the food grain. Surprisingly the Brahmin refused. To save one's life it was inappropriate to sacrifice another's, that too of a guest. There would be no redemption from sin.

But Kunti had her own view point. She felt an austere Brahmin should always be protected. She loved her son Bhim to distraction but was in awe of his valour and strength. She was confident that there was no one who would beat Bhim, leave alone the demon. She requested the Brahmin to not reveal their identity once the demon was overpowered and killed by her son.

Bhim wished to accomplish the feat on his own accord without enlisting the help of his brothers while they were away. Yudhisthira sensed something amiss. He disagreed with his mother's decision. She had agreed to sacrifice and abandon her own son for the sake of others.

Bhim was the strongest of the lot. Unlike Yudhisthira, Kunti had full faith in Bhim's valour and strength who she felt could never be defeated by any ordinary mortal. Moreover it is the duty of every individual to recognise and acknowledge the good others do to us and reciprocate the feelings when time and situation arises. She explained her stand on the situation.

Yudhisthira realised that his mother's decision had been driven by compassion and goodwill and not self gratification. But he asked his mother to tell the Brahmin to keep the news to himself lest they be discovered by their evil relations.

Bhim encountered the demon with ease. A tough fight ensued between the two. Both of great strength and energy rocked each other. But Bhim's movements were controlled and easy. The demon in contrast seemed to tire very easily. Sensing opportunity Bhim pinned him to the ground and tore him apart.

Hearing commotion, Baka's family came out of their dwelling. Bhim pacified them and asked them to abandon their violent ways lest they would face the same consequences. The residents of Ekachakra were dumb struck when they witnessed the superhuman feat. Baka lay lifeless, beaten and defeated on the ground. They wished to know the perpetrator of the noble deed. The Brahmin passed on all the credit to an unknown benevolent stranger. Kunti and her sons continued to live in Ekachakra in anonymity.

CHAPTER ELEVEN
Chaitraratha Parva

Kunti along with her sons continued to live in Ekachakra in the Brahmin's house. The boys studied the Vedas and other litterateur. Another Brahmin came to stay with them for a few days. He narrated stories and happenings in the neighbouring kingdoms. He narrated the events in the life of their great preceptor Drona.

DRONA AND DRUPADA

Bharadvaja a wise celibate Brahmin who lived on the banks of river Ganga. Once he beheld the beautiful damsel Gritachi, bathing. His desire got the better of him. He ejaculated. Later he collected his semen in a cup. From that was born his son Drona.

Bharadvaja was a good friend of king Prishata. His son Drupada too would come to the rishi's hermitage and spend hours playing with Drona. Both the boys were friends. After Prishata's death Drupada ascended the throne. In the meanwhile, Drona spent time studying the art of warfare and other texts. Once he learnt from someone that Parashurama, the great Brahmin warrior was leaving for the mountains and giving away the riches. Drona went up to him and asked for alms. Parashurama had given away all the material wealth he had to the needy except for his weapons.

Drona begged the great warrior to give him his weapons along with the knowledge of releasing and recalling them. His demand was accepted.

Drona moved ahead to meet his friend Drupada and ask for financial assistance. With a family to take care of it was getting difficult for Drona to make ends meet. Unfortunately Drupada was no longer the friend he had known in his childhood. Material wealth had clouded his vision. He was ashamed of Drona's austere status and did not wish to associate with him any longer. A king would like to be friends with a king and a learned man with another! Drupada declared pompously. This corroded Drona's heart to the core. Now besides learning he wished to make money to sustain. He dashed off straight to Hastinapur.

Drona had skills both intellectual and of a great warrior. In Hastinapur he took Bhishma's grandsons in his tutelage along with a lots of riches. The boys were trained to be brave warriors adept in the use of weapons. When the time arrived, the preceptor asked for a favour. Drupada had to be brought to dust. Mission undertaken by the students was successfully accomplished! Drupada along with his advisors was defeated, rounded up and taken as prisoner. Poetic justice was done. Drupada's kingdom was divided in two by Drona. Drona would be the king of the far flung southern land and Drona of the main northern part. Humiliation suffered at the hands of the Brahmin left Drupada miserable.

Drupada felt tormented. More so because Drona's kshatriya and intellectual powers were invincible. There was no way Drupada could match them. He felt helpless. Along with his wife, he set out on a journey in search of Brahmins who would pray at his behest for the birth of a valorous child. In future the child would supersede Drona in skills and defeat him.

YAJA AND UPAYAJA

Finally after a long search he came across two brothers' Yaja and Upayaja. Both the brothers were learned and rigid in vows. Drupada served both of them with great diligence. The younger one Upayaja was righteous and intelligent. He was a better candidate for performing sacrifices. Hence he was worshipped with more diligence by Drupada. When duly acquainted the king requested Upayaja to perform sacrifices for him that would give him an illustrious offspring who would kill Drona. In turn the Brahmin was offered a substantial amount of material wealth. Upayaja pondered over the request and advised the king to go to his elder brother Yaja.

Yaja never considered the merits of an action where material gains were involved. Drupada had no choice but to put forward the request to him though he had little respect for the older Brahmin. Yaja was pretty unscrupulous. Drupada was extremely angry at Drona. The Brahmin had belittled him over the issue of friendship. The king now wanted revenge. It appeared as though Drona was great Parasurama's clone who with his skills had razed all the kshatriyas from the face of earth. Moreover now he was the rich and powerful Kuru's preceptor. The Brahmin was promised a huge sum once the mission was accomplished.

Upayaja too came to assist the older brother. But there was no ulterior motive involved. He was a Brahmin and it was his duty to pray for the well being of others. Both the brothers prayed in unison. Both poured offerings in the sacrificial fire. Upayaja's incantations worked towards fulfilling the mission. But, unfortunately at the right time for consummation the queen was not prepared. But time and tide waits for none. The mission was accomplished without the queen.

The son born of the sacrificial offerings and prayers was a natural warrior, brave and talented who would spell doom on the enemy. The girl was dark, beautiful, energetic and goddess like. She was named Panchali. The Panchalas were extremely jubilant. It was foretold that the boy would be the cause of Drona's downfall and the girl would instil terror in the minds of the kshatriyas.

Queen Prishati was worried. Even though Panchali and her brother were not her biological children she still wanted to be known as their mother. The Brahmins agreed to bestow the boon on her. The elder Brahmin had received a lot of riches from the king. He was a happy man and agreed to return the favour. The son of Drupada was named Dhrishtadyumna. The daughter was called Krishna. Ironically Drona undertook the young prince Drishtadyumna in his own wings and became his preceptor. Splendid disciples would bring fame to Drona. Moreover destiny was inevitable. There was no point changing the course.

After hearing the account of Drupada and Drona from the Brahmin the Pandavs were agitated. Their past began to haunt them. Kunti sensed that. Very subtly she suggested that they now moved to a new place as they had, had enough of the beautiful town with mountains and green tall trees. She opined that Panchala, would be a good stopover, as it was known that king Yajnasena was a benevolent benefactor. Yudhisthira agreed to his mother's proposal but before committing talked about it to his younger brothers seeking their approval and opinion. The whole family thanked the Brahmin and decided to proceed to the city of Panchala.

Dvaipayna came to visit his grandsons often. He would enquire about their well being. At night he would tell them stories. Once a rishi had a very beautiful daughter. Unfortunately the father could not find a groom for the girl. The girl too prayed to the Almighty. She wished to be married to someone with infinite qualities. Strange request answered in a strange way! Since the proposition was simply impossible the lady had many husbands later. She had wanted only one but subconsciously asked God for many. Was Panchali's fate similar! Dvaipayna advised Kunti to move on to Panchala.

KING ANGARAPARNA

Once again the vanquished and disguised ones set out on a journey to the unknown. They started moving towards the north. After days of walking tirelessly they reached the holy river Ganga with Arjun in the lead to show the way. Gandharva king Angaraparna was sporting in the river waters with his wives. Gandharvas are considered to be stronger than men and have strong attachment for wealth and material things. The king was enraged at seeing strangers in the vicinity of his kingdom. He roared at them. He felt that the Ganges and the neighbouring forest Angaraparna was his private abode and no one dare set foot on its soil after sunset or rob and attack its residents. During the day the land was open for everyone. The king's tone was authoritative and threatening. He was proud of his strength.

Arjun was angry at the gandharva. How could anyone express ownership on the rivers and the forests! All the brothers were brave warriors and would not put up with wrongful oppression or comply with power. Only the weak submit to power. The holy Ganga takes human beings to heaven and bestows purity. It's sacred waters are accessible to everyone. This argument angered Angaraparna to no end. He challenged Arjuna to a duel.

Arjuna used the Agni weapon given to him by Drona. Merely skill would not have helped. He needed something divine. Angaraparna's chariot was charred by the impact of the missile and the king knocked down unconscious. His wife Kumbhinasi begged and pleaded for her own life and that of her husband. She wished to take refuge with the enemy.

Yudhishtra asked his brother to set the king free for he lay defeated on the ground and a woman was begging for his life. Surprisingly Angaraparna was in awe of the man who had charred his beautifully decorated chariot to ash. The warrior had granted the enemy his life. The gandharva wished to return the gratitude. He offered to give Arjuna well trained horses that galloped at the speed of light. He no longer took pride in his name and strength. Angaraparna after lots of penance had attained wisdom and insight and could see people around him as they were and not as how they appeared. He wished to pass on the knowledge to Yudhisthira. This knowledge made gandharvas superior to men.

Yudhisthira had forsaken Angaraparna's life for the sake of righteousness and not for personal gains. He refused the king's gifts. Angaraparna was now in awe. He wished to be their friend. In order not to belittle them he asked to be imparted the knowledge of releasing and recalling the Agni weapon and put a seal on friendship.

The Pandavs and Angaraparna were friends now. They were very open and forthright with each other. But some nagging questions had to be answered. The Pandavs had a reputation for being virtuous. They were always hard on the oppressive enemy. The boys wished to know as to why they were oppressed.

Angaraparna was well aware of the highly famed Kuru lineage. He was in awe of Drona. Drona was well versed in the Vedas and the science of weapons. Narada the devarshi always talked highly of their brave ancestors. He was aware of the parentage of the Pandavs. All of them had been born of rishis who were embodiment of virtue; Vayu, Shakra, and the Ashvins. Narada always talked of Yudhisthira and his younger brothers.

Angaraparna had only heard of them but never met them before. Moreover they hardly appeared to be the protégée of the illustrious lineage. Kings always travelled with a huge entourage with Brahmins in the forefront. So it was not difficult to recognise a king from an ordinary man. Yudhisthira and his brothers themselves looked like wandering ascetics. Moreover a man finds it difficult to keep his cool once he is challenged in the presence of his wife. Gandharvas were a strong powerful race. Their strength is at its nadir after sunset. But the Pandavs high in the knowledge of arms and at the same time in Vedas were the strongest of the lot. They were enlightened Brahmins in their own right.

Kings were always guided and advised by priests. The priest appointed too needed to be a scholar and not the one driven by desire for material gratification. With right direction and advice, the king was capable of conquering the whole earth.

SAMVARANA AND TAPATI

In the course of conversation the gandharva had addressed them as Tapatya. But they were called Kounteya, sons of Kunti. They were intrigued. The gandharva explained thus; King Vivasvat had a beautiful daughter Tapati. She was unparalleled in learning and qualities. He wished to find a husband for her who equalled her qualities. King Samvarana of the Kuru lineage appeared to be the right person to be her husband. The king was benevolent towards his subjects but was a scorcher of enemies. He had great virtues and qualities.

Once Samvarana went hunting in the forest. He beheld the beautiful Tapati frolicking. He was overcome with desire. He went in search of the beauty. But she appeared to have disappeared in a flash among the foliage. The king now had eyes only for the girl. They were always looking for her everywhere. He was in love. He was no longer the brave one in control. He was lovelorn constantly in search of the damsel. Tapati too was stricken with love for the handsome Samvarana.

Gathering her wits she approached Samvarana and confessed her love for him. The king asked her to marry him according to gandharva rites. Tapati had reservations. She was under the care and supervision of her father and was in no position to take decisions independently. She suggested that he went to her father and impress upon him his worthiness as a suitor. Samvarana was stumped. How was he going to ask the great Vivasvat, as brilliant as Sun himself, for his daughter's hand! Would Vivasvat consider him worthy enough to be his daughter's husband! Nagging thoughts robbed the king of his senses.

In the meantime his ministers and a retinue of soldiers came searching for him. Samvarana was without his horse, lying on the ground, weak and not his usual self. They were full of remorse. One of the wise ministers, felt that the monarch had lost sense of direction while on a hunting spree and was hungry and exhausted. Everyone was sent back except for this minister who stayed back to nurse.

Samvarana went up to the mountaintop praying day and night to the Sun god. His heart and mind were no longer in his control. The brilliant rishi Vashishtha happened to observe all the activities that had been taking place. Through wisdom and insight he knew that Samvarana was suffering from pangs of love. Convinced of the king's sincerity, love and magnanimity he decided to play cupid. He went to Vivasvat to ask for Tapati's hand on Samvarana's behalf.

On recommendations from the illustrious rishi the king did not think twice. He felt that there would be no better husband than the one suggested by Vashistha for his daughter. With the blessings of her father Tapati co joined with Samvarana in holy matrimony. The couple were besotted to one another. Desire and passion got the better of the king. He spent all his time with his wife enchanted and in a trance.

The king is the head of the state. But somehow in the pursuit of happiness Samvarana seemed to have forgotten his duties. With the passage of time the once prosperous state started moving towards ruin. Samvarana realised his folly. He had neglected his state and subjects for long. Lord Indira had refused to pour blessings on his kingdom. People started dying of hunger and starvation. Samvarana and Tapati were rebuked by Vashishtha. Embarrassed the couple turned their attention to the duties they owed to their people. The subjects again got their king back. Beholding their sacrifices. The whole kingdom was rejuvenated. Samvarana and Tapati became parents to a valiant son Kuru. Born of the radiant Tapati, Kurus were also called Tapatya. Curiosity quenched!

VISHVAMITRA AND VASHISHTHA

But now Pandavs were intrigued by the mention of rishi Vashishtha who was their ancestor's preceptor. Angaraparna shared the knowledge he had. Vashishtha's acrimony with Vishvamitra was not unfounded and without basis. Vishvamitra's father Gadhi ruled over Kanyakubja. His son was valorous, looked after his huge armies and spent time hunting in the forest. Once on an expedition in the forest, Vishvamitra tired and exhausted, stopped over at Vashishtha's hermitage for food. The rishi served the brave one and his entourage with honour. For dessert there was milk as sweet as ambrosia from his favourite cow. Out of lust for all the good things in life and arrogance, Vishvamitra wished to take the cow Nandini with him. In turn he offered Vashishtha a substantial amount of wealth. But the Brahmin had no inkling towards wealth. The cow's milk was used to gratify ancestors and guests. The Brahmin did not wish to part with her.

Unfortunately Vashishtha had no choice but to let her go. But the cow refused to budge and leave the hermitage. Stubbornly she just refused to give in. Vishvamitra's attendants started losing patience. They took to beating her with sticks. The cow bellowed in pain. The king used his kshatriya energy of force and the Brahmin of tolerance and forbearance. The soldiers now forcibly tried to drag the calf. Anger and desire, the two invincible vices were Vashishtha's slaves; even though they are overlord of great men and women. Witnessing so much of violence on the humble cow and her calf corroded the rishi's heart but he did not let anger engulf him.

The traumatised cow appeared to question her master's silence. He loved her and her pain was his. Apparently the pain of her master and of her calf propelled Nandini to use her strength and energy. She charged at Vishvamitra's army like a bull in frenzy. This frightened the soldiers to no end. There was panic and chaos. Off went the entourage spinning in all directions. No one dared to come near Nandini and her calf. But in spite of the stampede none lost life.

This was the turning point in Vishvamitra's life. It was time for retrospection. The Brahmin without an army had defeated his all powerful force. True power arose from renunciation. He gave up his throne and became an ascetic. Vishvamitra's encounter with Vashishtha did not end there. More was still to come.

KING KALMASHAPADA

Vishvamitra's ego had been badly bruised. King Kalmashapada had great prowess and was the ruler of the earth. He contemplated anointing either Vashishita or Vishvamitra as the royal priest. Once on a hunting spree he crossed swords with Shakti, Vashishtha's son.

While coming from the opposite direction he refused to give way to the king and his entourage. This enraged Kalmashapada. But this was within the precincts of law. In hierarchy the Brahmin always came before the king. The king in arrogance abused Shakti.

The Brahmin had done no wrong and was humble and kind. Kalmashapada lacked values with his life full of pleasure and lust. Vishvamitra happened to pass by wherein the two were fighting. He hid himself from their view. He wished to be the officiating priest of Kalmashapada and at the same time wanted to settle scores with Vashishtha whom he envied for his intellectual powers. The king was being disrespectful towards Shiva. The young ascetic told Kalmashapada that his life would be like that of demon Kimkara. Kimkara was powerful and strong, ate flesh of animals and had no human instincts. His soul was tormented by his unholy deeds and ways of life. The bitter but true words frightened Kalmashapada. He cajoled and requested the rishi to be merciful towards him.

But Shakti like his father was no ordinary being. He could see through the king's soul. His prediction was in keeping with his deep insight. The king had no respect for the learned Brahmins. Once a hungry Brahmin came his way and begged for food. Kalmashapada in arrogance asked the cook to serve whatever was there in the kitchen; flesh of an animal. The hungry Brahmin's heart repulsed at the sight of the food; but Kalmashapada felt no remorse or regret at his cruel act. He was of the opinion that the powers of a kshatriya were greater than the powers of a Brahmin. To prove his point he killed Vashishtha's son Shakti and then eliminated all his brothers.

Like a mute spectator, Vishvamitra had all this while witnessed the events that unfolded. He felt he had defeated Vashishita emotionally. The death of his sons would provoke Vashishita into a duel which he would never win from a kshatriya. But Vishvamitra though now a sage himself had not fathomed the power of learning which the rishi had mastered.

By now Vashishita knew that Vishvamitra and the king had conspired to kill his sons. He was full of remorse and a broken man. But he never sought to take revenge on the evil two. In his state of utter grief he did a couple of times tried to take his own life. Every time he returned back to his hermitage, tired and exhausted. He had lived there with his sons. Their absence haunted him. He felt tormented. He would set out again and again only to return back. But fortunes and times change.

Shakti's wife Adrishyanti was expecting her dead husband's child. Vashistha felt alive and happy after a very long time. He wished to live again. He would see his son again in his grandson. His heart was no longer desolate. A child would fill the void left by his sons.

Adrishyanti once accompanied by Vashishta came across Kalmapasada. She was mortified. He would now eliminate the remaining family too! Vashishta allayed her fears and asked her to be calm; for no evil would emanate from the once evil king. The death of innocent Brahmins at his hands had corroded Kalmapasada's inner being. It made him lose his inner being and peace of mind. Regret, guilt, fear and remorse unshackled his senses. He had eliminated Shakti and his brothers as radiant as sun. It was like Rahu had swallowed the sun and caused an eclipse. But twelve long years of suffering and remorse had evolved Ketu, a shining star. He begged for forgiveness and redemption from sin. Casting his grief aside the magnanimous one performed his duty. He forgave the sinner.

Kalmapasada appointed Vashistha as his preceptor. He was wiser and older. He paid obeisance to Brahmins and ruled over his subjects benevolently. He asked Vashishita for a boon in order to continue his lineage. The king wanted a child as brilliant and virtuous as the

Brahmin. Vashistha always righteous and benevolent agreed to the request. He accompanied the kshatriya to his capital, Ayodhya.

The beautiful city and its subjects welcomed the radiant ones. It looked like Amravati, Indra's capital recreated. When the time was appropriate the queen co joined with Vashistha. The king with gratitude thanked the illustrious one who later returned to his hermitage. Rajarshi Ashmaka was born thus who founded the city of Potana.

Adrishyanti became mother to son Parashar. Vashishtha in the absence of his son took upon himself the role of a father. The boy fondly addressed him thus. When the child was old enough his mother told him the truth. This had a deep impact on Parashar's mind. It robbed him of his childhood. He was no longer naive and innocent. His heart was full of venom and revenge. He wished to eliminate all kshatriyas from the face of earth. But Vashistha in all sincerity hoped that Parashara did not tread the path of destruction. He tried to explain to him his point of view and not impose his will.

KING KRITAVIRYA

Vashishta narrated to his grandson the story of king Kritavirya. Being benevolent and kind the king gave away lots of riches to the Brahmins. They all belonged to the Brighu race. With the passage of time the king passed through the final journey on earth. Destiny is unpredictable. Meanwhile, Kritavirya's descendants fell upon bad times and the brahmins became rich and prosperous. Like beggars, they asked the Brahmins for their riches back. Afraid of losing their wealth they buried it in the ground. When Kritavirya's descendants learnt of the deception, the treasure was dug out. The enraged kshatriyas went on a rampage. They decimated the Brighu race. No one was left; men, children, women, and even expecting mothers.

One of the women managed to escape with her unborn child in her womb. With the passage of time the radiant Ourva illuminated the earth. He was brave and strong. In the course of time, kshatriyas learnt of the presence of a Brighu descendant on earth. They felt intimidated. They were paralysed with fear. They were well aware of their evil act against the Brighu Brahmins. Every possible precaution had been taken to eliminate the entire clan. The news of a survivor left them gasping for breath. The boy was sure to avenge the death of his race.

A Brahmin's revenge was the most lethal where the blow never missed the target. Having lost their power to think and see things in the right perspective the frightened Kshatriyas approached Ourva's mother and sought redressal. The lady felt no malice as time had healed her wounds but Ourva was unforgiving and unrelenting.

He was a Brahmin and not a kshatriya. Killing human beings was no mean job for him. But being a Brahmin he had to dispense justice. The kshatriyas as instructed by his mother begged for forgiveness and redemption. Ourva accepted their sincere apologies and set them free from his curse. But greater destruction was in store. He wanted to char everyone to death. The Brighu Brahmins had done no wrong. But mankind had treated them shabbily. He just wished to take away everyone's life. He was full of anger.

One day while asleep Ourva had a strange vision. His ancestors' were discussing as to why they had hidden the treasure from the kshatriyas. Apparently they had lived long, austere, hard lives and no longer wished to live anymore. But taking away one's own life is a sin. So they hid the riches which were of no use to the frugal ones in order to create enmity with the kshatriyas. The killer would be damned and the victim would attain heavens. Subtly the ancestors were urging him against being a sinner for lack of direction and perception. The Brighus were never weak and powerless nor the kshatriyas the oppressors. Having heard as to what his forefathers had to say Ourva was full of remorse.

His anger seemed to haunt him. On one hand was the revelation of no injustice and on the other hand was the brutality of the kshatriyas inflicted on the Brahmins. The king could have prevented it but he did nothing about it. Ourva was now calm and serene like the ocean.

Parashar did not wish to upset his ageing grandfather with his stubbornness and disrespect. An agitated mind loses out on dharma, artha and kama. Vashishtha advised Parashar to cast aside his venom for that would take him to the path of destruction. With his grandfather in attendance he performed fire sacrifices praying for the destruction of demons. Shakti and his brothers as destined were freed from the suffering called earth and were enjoying company of gods. Vashistha with his insight knew that evil would meet its end. Parashar was just an instrument. The great sages requested Parashar to end his sacrifice. As advised by the elders he threw the fire in the forest. Forest fires are known to burn even today symbolising death of evil.

Yudhisthira were intrigued as to why king Kalmapasada requested Vashishita to help him beget a progeny; and vice versa why did Vashishta agree to unite with a woman other than his wife. The king under the influence of evil often went hunting in the forest mindlessly. Once in arrogance he became the death knell of another Brahmin who left the world without a progeny. His wife in anger and remorse cursed the king and pronounced that a similar fate would befall him. The Brahmin wife's curse began to haunt him. As fate would have it, he had no one else but Vashishita to fall back on. He requested Vashishta to unite with his wife at the right time of the season.

CHAPTER TWELVE
Draupadi Svayamvara Parva

King Angaraparna and the Pandavs were friends now. Yudhisthira wished to have a preceptor who was well versed in Vedas and whose insight and guidance would help them get back their lost kingdom and fortunes. As suggested by Angaraparna they moved towards a place of pilgrimage in the forest. There they met rishi Dhoumya in his hermitage. The Brahmin was the most appropriate person for the position of a preceptor. Dhoumya accepted the proposition without much thought. He considered the Pandavs as kings incarnate for they were intelligent, valorous and patient. They were bound to get their throne back with their strength of character.

Arjuna gifted Angaraparna the agneya weapon but refused to take anything in return. Very humbly he promised to ask for help whenever the need arose.

Yudhisthira along with his brothers and Dhoumya in the forefront moved towards Panchala. On their way they were joined by fellow Brahmins. They were also going in the same direction. Apparently there was a massive event organised by the king. It was the svayamvara of his daughter Panchali. The king had invited kings and princes of neighbouring states to participate. Actors, dancers, bards, wrestlers too were invited to entertain guests. The guests were mighty and rich and were likely to give away lots of wealth to Brahmins seeking blessings and victory. Panchali was Drupada's daughter born after lots of prayers and sacrifices. She was mighty Dhrishtadyumna's sister. The lady was a blazing beauty in her own right and intelligent.

The Brahmins invited Arjun and his brothers to join them. Since they were strong and handsome, one of them was bound to be the lucky suitor, they joked. They moved to the south of Panchala which was ruled by Drupada. In Panchala they were visited by their grandfather Dvaipayana. On his advice they set out towards Drupada's palace. A humble potter's abode became theirs, where they lived as austere Brahmins who sustained on alms. Drupada always dreamt of his friend Pandu's son Arjun as a husband for his daughter. He expected his future son in law to be a skilled warrior. For this he had a heavy bow carved out and an equally unattainable target to hit. Drupada announced the svayamvara of his daughter open. Duryodhan too participated accompanied by his friend Karna. Drupada warmly welcomed the citizens, brahmins and the contestants with reverence.

A huge platform was built. The meeting place was enclosed in a moat and then surrounded by a wall. A beautiful canopy was placed on the top. The place was surrounded by tiny palaces for the princes to rest. Musical instruments echoed in the background. The princes were seated on the royal seats. The Pandavs took seats with the Brahmins. Panchali all bathed and adorned in beautiful clothes and jewellery arrived. Ghee was poured in the sacrificial fire by the Brahmins present.

Dhrishtadyumna spelled the rules at the beginning of the contest. Every participant had to hit a designated target. Five arrows and a bow were provided. The arrow had to pass through an aperture before reaching the target. Draupadi was introduced to the participants and their achievements recounted. Karna was inseparable from his friend Duryodhan so that justified his presence. Sons of king of Gandhara with Shakuni in the lead too participated. Warriors' Ashvatthama and Bhoja wished to be the lucky ones.

A brother vied with another brother for Draupadi's hand. To witness the svayamvara, a huge assembly of great beings arrived from different walks of life. Balaram and Krishna of the Vrishnis and the Andhakas were not to be left behind. Krishna was the only one to recognise the Pandavs in disguise. One after the other participating princes arrived exhibiting valour. For most the bow was too heavy to lift and for the motley crowd who managed to overcome the first hurdle stringing was not possible. All of them felt dejected and humiliated. Each ridiculed the other.

ARJUN CLAIMS HIS BRIDE

When none of the kshatriya could make it, Arjun moved towards the arena. The Brahmins present were aghast and agitated. An austere fragile Brahmin was inappropriate for a kshatriyas feat. Most likely he was bound to lose. This would bring dishonour to the race. But some wise ones could see through Arjun's frugal bearing. He was strong and muscular. A Brahmin could do all that other varnas could not. Even after living on air, water and fruits in difficult times he would still maintain his strength with his inner energy. Arjuna went up on the platform. According to rites he circumambulated the arrow. Then effortlessly he picked it up, strung it and shot down the target. The assembly present cheered loudly. Bards sang paeans in praise of the hero. Yudhisthira along with his other brothers left the assembly unrecognised. Draupadi went up to the hero and garlanded him. The Brahmins too showered blessings on the unsung hero.

Drupada was a happy man. He addressed the assembly and announced that he would marry of his daughter to the great Brahmin who had met the challenge. The verdict added fuel to fire. The kings and princes had already been left red faced. A Brahmin had managed to usurp their title. To add insult to injury the father had decided to give his daughter to the austere Brahmin in marriage. Svayamvara was meant only for kshatriyas and not for Brahmins, they argued. A Brahmin, because of his varna, per se, was not qualified to contest. It was against the law. The father and daughter, after much of hospitality were showing disrespect for the kshatriyas assembled there. All the fallen heroes fumed.

The kings and princes with their badly bruised egos turned violent. They wished to throw Panchali in the sacrificial fire and simply kill Drapuda. They were equally furious at the Brahmin. But killing a Brahmin would incur sin. A Brahmin is the preceptor of the kshatriyas who guides them. All their riches and adulations are because of his prayers.

The mob of royals with their arms raised and clad in armour rushed towards Drupada in unison. In turn the ageing monarch totally taken unawares and scared to death took refuge behind the brothers Arjun and Bhim. Bhim very carelessly and without any tangible effort uprooted a tree and held it in his hand like a staff. He stood guard next to his brother protecting him from any harm that came his way.

Vasudev was the one who with his insight recognised Bhim and Arjuna in the guise of Brahmins. He sensed that no one else but Arjun alone had the ability to hold a long heavy bow effortlessly. Only Bhim had the strength to uproot a tree. The calm and serene but tiger like Brahmin who had left the assembly would have to be none else but Yudhisthira. The two handsome youth Nakul and Sahdev were born of Ashvins.

It was now a known fact in the neighbouring kingdoms that the Pandavs along with their mother had escaped from the house of lac.

Vasudev shared the news with his older brother Balaram. Both the brothers were ecstatic at the prospect that their father's sister Kunti being possibly alive. Arjun and Bhim fell on the enraged mob like two mad elephants. They were very confident and enjoying the confrontation without fear. They instructed all the Brahmins to stand aside and watch the spectacle while they repulsed the angry kings and princes.

Arjuna picked up the bow he had received in the svayamvara. From the other side Karna was in the forefront leading the mob. It is considered permissible to fight a Brahmin who is willing to put up a fight! Shalya, king of Madra attacked Bhim and Karna lugged at Arjun. Seeing the enemy approach Arjuna released three arrows injuring Karna. On regaining composure he immediately levelled a counter attack. Blows after blows followed in quick succession. By now Karna was completely in awe of the Brahmin. He chose to withdraw from the battle. He knew that the apparent Brahmin was no ordinary mortal but an incarnation of Parasurama who was an authority on Dhanur veda. The Brahmin's prowess was invincible. He had effortlessly picked up the bow, strung it and shot the arrow where other great kshatriyas had failed miserably.

Bhim and Shalya were engaged in a duel on the other hand. Each hit out at the other with venom. Both were of unparallel strength. Finally Bhim lifted Shalya, swung him high in the air and hurled him on the ground taking care not to kill as this was not a battle ground. The Brahmin boys were the hero of the event. They were accepted as supreme and invincible by everyone present. There was lots of curiosity about their lineage; they had performed some superhuman feats else Karna and Shalya would never be intimidated.

Vasudev now was certain that the Brahmins present were none other than the Pandavs. Most likely they were in disguise to dodge

Duryodhan and death. Very slyly Krishna dissuaded the assembly from delving deep into their background lest they be discovered and attacked again. Panchali had found her soulmate in a Brahmin and was happy, he reasoned. It was time the kings and princes went back home. Vasudev brilliantly diverted everyone's attention from the heroes in hiding.

Amidst fanfare and applause Bhim and Arjuna along with Draupadi left for home. Kunti was always worried for her sons when they were away. There was possible danger always lurking in the background, be it in the form of Duryodhan and his brothers or evil that would use illusion to deceive. Arjun announced their arrival to his mother on reaching home. As a habitual exercise she asked him to distribute alms equally among themselves.

Kunti immediately realised her folly. One should think before saying something. Words once released cannot be taken back; the process is irreversible. But Kunti's words changed the course of her sons' lives. Draupadi was to be the wife to all the brothers! But Yudhisthira suggested that only Arjun married Draupadi since he had participated in the svayamvara. But Arjun did not want his mother to be in an awkward position and her words negated. For them she personified dharma. Yudhisthira in the meantime realised that many women in the household were bound to create a rift. It was best decided by him that they all married Draupadi. The decision was taken keeping in mind the welfare of the whole family. Mother's position and words were respected. All the brothers were happy with his decision.

In the meantime, Vasudev and Balarama too came wandering to the potter's house in search of their cousins. Their doubts were allayed when they saw Kunti and Draupadi with the rest. They humbly out of reverence touched Kunti's feet. Yudhisthira was intrigued as to how the brothers managed to track them down. But Krishna was no ordinary mortal. He was epitome of wisdom. Shortly both left lest the Pandav's identity be exhumed.

Dhrishtadyumna was worried and apprehensive regarding Draupadi's welfare. He followed the Brahmins who had left with her. He hid himself safely from everyone's view. From a distance he saw that the Brahmins after reaching home had handed over the alms to their mother. The lady then instructed Draupadi to make the first offerings to Brahmins and divide the rest in two halves. One was for Bhim who was big and huge and the second half for his other brothers. At night all the brothers rolled out on the grass with their mother making bed in the direction of their heads and wife towards their feet. They discussed great wars and warriors before going to sleep.

Drupada felt miserable for he had failed as a father. He knew nothing about the lineage of the Brahmins who had married his daughter. They could either be Vaishya's or Shudras or possibly be Kshatriyas. He was grieved over the thought of his daughter breaking bread with members of a lower strata. But his sombre mood changed to ecstasy at the thought of his daughter's possibility of being married to a Pandav.

Dhrishtadyumna hurried back home. He recounted to his father, "the boys were blessed by their chief priest Dyoumna. They went back home to a potter's house. A old lady sat surrounded by three more Brahmins. The lady possibly was their mother and the three men their brothers. The two paid homage to their mother and asked Draupadi to do so. All the five then set out to beg for alms. Their conversation centred around battles. They were in all likelihood high class kshatriyas. There were murmurs in the royalty that the Pandavs had escaped from the house of lac".

Draupada rushed his priest to his daughter's marital home. He was extremely agitated. His mind was in turmoil. The priest requested Arjun to come out clear with his lineage and varna. The king had a strong premonition that they were his dead friend Pandu's sons. The brothers humbly paid homage to the priest. Yudhisthira wished that the king did not regret his decision. Being a father, he had set high standards for a prospective groom for his daughter. His brother with his skill, knowledge and perseverance had achieved an unattainable feat. A weakling or someone not skilled in the use of arms would never have achieved the assigned target. All these accomplishments were much higher than lineage, varna and intentions. It was best for the king to not confuse and torture himself with petty issues but look at the larger picture.

CHAPTER THIRTEEN
Vaivahika Parva

Arjun along with his family was invited by Drupada over a lavish feast assigned to future in laws of his daughter. Chariots drawn by brilliant horses were sent to fetch the guests. Dhouyma was placed ahead of the party with Draupadi and Kunti in the following chariots. All the brothers followed hence in separate carriages.

The king in turmoil devised ways and means of ascertaining the lineage of the Brahmin whom Draupadi was to marry. He put up a huge display of equipments used by different varnas; fruits, garlands, cattle ropes, objects used in agriculture, chariots, horses, armour, spears, arrows, catapults etc used in wars. There were objects created by craftsmen and so on.

On reaching the palace Kunti and Draupadi were directed to the inner quarters where the queen resided. Both the women were received with utmost respect. The ladies present there paid homage to Kunti. The Pandavs were welcomed warmly by the king's sons, advisors, relations and attendants. After a delicious meal Drupada showed them the display he had got installed. His endeavour was fruitful. Yudhisthira and his brothers showed keen interest in bows, arrows and javelins. This reinforced his belief in their designated varna. Draupada could no longer hold back his curiosity. He had imagined and made enough of wild guesses. The suspense and uncertainty were killing him. He wished to know their identity. Whether they were kshatriyas or vaishyas or in worst case scenario shudras or possibly Brahmins as they appeared to be! He humbly requested them to be honest as that was the highest virtue, even higher than sacrifices and charity.

DISGUISED YUDHISTHIRA REVEALS HIS IDENTITY

Yudhisthira now convinced of Drupada's integrity revealed it all; his family's escape from the house of lac and life henceforth. He revealed his parentage and links to Bharata dynasty. He talked of his uncle Dhritrashtra's partial leaning towards Duryodhan and his other sons. The humiliation and hurt the elders had suffered because of the collective shortcomings of both the father and son. How they had been victims of Duryodhan's conniving and vicious temperament!

Yudhisthira humbly requested Drupada to be their preceptor. The king formally invited Yudhisthira and his entire family to come and stay in the palace in Panchala. He assured them of all possible help in their effort to restore their lost kingdom back. Draupada wanted to kill two birds with one stone. He wished to settle scores with one time friend Drona with the help of skilful Pandavs and help Draupadi's husband Arjun win back the throne so that she would be the queen.

Now it was time Draupadi formally got married. As decided by Kunti all the brothers were to marry the princess. The news came as a thunderbolt for Drupada though he never once doubted Yudhisthira's and Kunti's intentions. He had not heard of that type of alliance before. The path of Dharma is extremely subtle, reasoned Yudhisthira. The worried father's mind was still in turmoil. Luckily for everyone grandfather Dvaipayna arrived to find answers to the dilemma that puzzled Drupada.

Krishna Dvaipayna in all humbleness was asked to discourse on the pertinent issue. He was the highest authority on Vedas and learning. This practice has become obsolete over a period of time but was prevalent in the past, opined the sage. Dvaipayna did not wish to impose his will. Drupada found the idea of a woman with many husbands a sin. Dhrishtadyumna considered a man consorting with his younger brother's wife against the norms of Dharma. Yudhisthira counter argued that Jatila, a virtuous damsel consorted with seven sages. There was no higher preceptor than a mother and it was his mother's inner voice which commanded them to share.

Vyasa after listening patiently to everyone wished to talk to Drupada alone. Draupada was the father and his acceptance of the situation mattered the most. Vyasa tried to explain as to how, a woman's marriage to many men was acceptable. It went thus. Yama performed fire sacrifices in the forests, praying for the death and destruction of animals that had gone extremely violent and would kill innocents without provocation. As a result men started living long becoming almost immortal. Immortality brings with it lots of pride and venom.

The immortal lord Indra beheld a beautiful lotus in a pond. He was shaken and enraged. Besides him who else had the power to water the earth! Swiftly he tried to trace the source. He went flying over the mighty Ganges. Ultimately he reached the snow covered Himalayan peaks. He was raking with envy and anger. He shouted out aloud, "I am invincible. I am the king." The mighty peaks appeared to mock his hollow claims. He slowly realised he was going limp. The rain droplets, he was bestowing were flowing in caverns and turning into solid ice. He was no longer the powerful Indra but hard mass of ice lying lifeless and worthless. He begged the lord to show him road to salvation. With his venom he had given death to scores of men and women on earth so he would have to be a part of humans on earth. Indra would have to flow through the womb of Ganges before it could rise again in its celestial home. This would be the path to salvation.

Vyasa compared the Pandavs to Indra lying dormant and powerless. He felt Draupadi was the lotus who would instigate them to get their energies and aura back and fight evil and be their partner in the holy mission. All the six were not ordinary human beings. He urged Vasudev and Balarama his brother to be seen in the same light, divine. Drupada touched Vyasa's feet out of reverence. Further, Vyasa narrated to the anxious father the story of the rishi who had a beautiful daughter. The damsel prayed for a husband with every possible quality on earth. She was blessed with five godly husbands. It appeared as though Draupadi's fate was similar to the lady's.

Drupada soon realised that destiny was the king. It is preordained. Accepting the situation wholeheartedly without rancour, he set out to prepare for his daughter's wedding, inviting friends and family. The Pandavs dressed in royal clothes befitting princes and kings, adorned with jewels. Dhoumya poured offerings in the sacrificial fire and chanted holy verses. The first to be married was Yudhisthira. He walked hand in hand with Draupadi around the sacrificial fire. The younger ones followed suit. Drupada loaded all his son-in-laws with gifts; chariots, gold, horses, elephants, servants and wealth. He bestowed alms on the poor, seeking blessings for his daughter's happy future. The Pandavs made Draupada's palace their abode. Drupada was now an emotionally strong man with so many strong warriors by his side. He now feared just no one. Women of the household came and paid homage to Kunti. Kunti blessed Draupadi after the wedding. She wished that she be the mother to brave valorous sons. She hoped that Draupadi would be the queen of Kurujangala in future and wife to husbands who would conquer the earth. Even Krishna loaded them with gifts. Yudhisthira, accepted all the gifts to strengthen their friendship with Krishna.

CHAPTER FOURTEEN
Viduragama

The news of emergence of Pandavs in the guise of Brahmins reached Hastinapur. There were rumours that Bhim had tormented the powerful king Shalya and Arjuna had accepted Drupada's challenge and succeeded. Arjun and Bhim had proved their mettle as unparalleled warriors. The citizens denigrated Bhishma and Dhritrashtra for not reining Duryodhan.

Duryodhan was devastated. Moreover the beautiful Draupadi choosing austere skilful Brahmins over brave rich kshatriya kings hurt his pride. Even worse was the fact that the cousins had found a powerful ally in Drupada. The thought of Draupadi's strong brothers Dhristadyumna and Shikandi gave him nightmares.

PANDAVS RETURN; DHRITRASHTRA'S NIGHTMARE BEGINS

Vidura on the other hand was very happy. Duryodhan, his friend Karna and maternal uncle Shakuni had been left red faced by none other than the Pandavs who were wronged from the time they had landed in Hastinapur. Vidhura announced Draupadi's wedding to the Kuru heir. Dhritrashtra got duped into thinking that the groom was his son, Duryodhan. He was over joyous. On learning the truth his jubilation turned to sorrow. He was overwhelmed with fear. His son would create a havoc. Earlier Dhritrashtra had to lose out on the throne and now in a twist of fate Duryodhan would have to step aside for the cousins who were protected by destiny. Moreover Pandavs would now have lots of powerful allies who were likely to strengthen them. Dhritrashtra was certain that his son would never be able to take it with dignity. He was filled with anxiety.

Dhritrashtra put up on a facade as not to betray his inner turmoil to Bhishma, Drona and Vidura. He expressed extreme happiness and rejoiced. Duryodhan reprimanded him. He commanded his father to continue with their enmity and devise means of weakening them. Else their strength, valour and intelligence would dislodge them from the throne. He instructed the family to be united in his endeavour. Dhritrashtra being a father did not wish to lose out on his son's love and affection. He assured him that his expression of love and interest was reserved only for his children and not even his dead brother's sons. He asked Duryodhan and Karna to devise ways of eliminating Yudhisthira's claims to the throne. He assured Duryodhan that the mask of happiness was to deceive Bhishma and Vidura who would be a source of impediment to their plan.

Duryodhan was now a man on a mission. He thought of tempting Drupada with gifts and wealth so that he abandoned Yudhisthira. If that plan failed he had another up his sleeve. The Pandavs strength would diminish if a rift arose between sons of Kunti and sons of Madri. A rift in the family would weaken the brothers or still better create differences among all. Or killing Bhim slyly would weaken Arjun who was his partner in duels and hence weaken all. Else Draupadi if instigated against her husbands would prove to be the ammunition of destruction. The best way to fight Yudhisthira was not through skill and strength but with deception, he opined. Duryodhan stooped real low in desperation. He wished to tempt the boys with lustful women. This would lead them to the path of debauchery. Eventually it would break them away from Draupadi and her father Drupada. The game plan was to break their alliance and trust with powerful Drupada before the bond got too strong. He wished to see them all dead and buried for his peace of mind. He was intimidated and could not think rationally.

But Karna felt insulted. He had confidence in his skill and valour. He urged Duryodhan to be a man enough and defeat his cousins with bravery which was every kshatriyas weapon. A kshatriya would never lay down his weapon before the battle. It was shameful for the race. Moreover using deceit would not help Duryodhan win since Pandavs had become strong with lots of powerful allies. They were no longer children who could be oppressed as they had come of age with lots of hardships and sufferings. Trying to create alienation from allies and among themselves would never work. The wise Drupada respected their skill over lineage and wealth. Now that they had it all, nothing would turn him and his daughter against them. Since his daughter was married to them he would help them in every possible way to get the share of their father's kingdom. He would never desert Yudhisthira no matter whatever the temptation.

Karna was not afraid of Arjun's skill. He advised Duryodhan against using deception. Karna thought it best to go and fight Yudhisthira on Panchala's home turf. It was most likely that their cousin Vasudev, would leave no stone unturned, whether it was sacrificing riches or his own kingdom for Kunti's sons. The most logical thing to do was to bring Drupada along with his sons and son-in-laws to dust even before Vasudev joined hands with them. A kshatriya needed to follow the dictates of dharma which is of valour and not of deception. He asked Duryodhan to mobilize his huge army and get ready to attack. After all winning them over with gifts or by not agreeing to their terms and conditions of handing over the kingdom according to laws of inheritance would not work.

Dhritrashtra too approved of Karna's point of view. But before coming to any logical conclusion he wanted to discuss the matter with Bhishma, Drona and Vidura. Even his ancestors had ruled the entire earth with valour. Bhishma refuted the idea of going to war without a second thought. A part of the kingdom belonged to Pandav's deceased father so they were the lawful inheritors. Hence it needed to be handed over to them with respect and honour. Otherwise any intention of depriving them of their rightful share would bring dishonour to the family. Ironically earlier he had to step aside and make way for Pandu, mused Dhritrashtra. Destiny had treated his son in a similar fashion. Dhritrashtra was wallowing in self pity and was blinded by love for his children. Bhishma visualized the situation with utmost honesty.

Bhishma felt stripped of authority and integrity for letting Duryodhan drive away Pandavs from Hastinapur so that he could be crowned in their absence. Drona expressed solidarity with Bhishma's opinion. It was time the Kurus apologised for the wrong that had transpired and made amends. It was time the share of their inheritance be handed over to them without any obstacle. Yudhisthira needed to be welcomed with full honour as the future king.

Karna's wounds were still raw. He had to beat a hasty retreat in Draupadi's swayamvara when face to face with Arjuna. Drona and Bhishma's advice only added fuel to fire. He wanted to see Arjun and his brothers weakened on all fronts to salvage his fledgling ego. Duryodhan too would never think of sharing the kingdom which he considered his own especially with someone whom he hated to his heart's content. He had an emotional anchor in his friend Karna.

Karna lashed out at Bhisma and Drona. They had sustained on Dhritrashtra's riches and bread practically all their life. Their advice was apparently good but not in favour of the man who had nurtured them. Dhritrashtra had been breeding snakes in his backyard, he spat.

Besieged by emotions Karna started exalting the virtues of a friend. A true friend he said gave no such advice which went against his ally. No one can bring us happiness or misery for they are predestined. The elders' sagacious advice was incapable of bringing any solace to anyone.

Karna, then recounted the tale of king Ambuvicha who ruled over Magadha. He was a man without any skill. But fortunately for him, he had an able minister Mahakarni. With the passage of time, sensing the king's fallibility Mahakarni started exalting in self worth. He coveted Ambuvicha's wealth and women. Desires are like horses without reins. Finally he wanted to settle for nothing less but his kingdom. But that was not his destiny even though he was pitched against a weak being. Having said all Karna wanted Dhritrashtra to decide for himself as to who his friends were.

Drona lost his cool on hearing Karna talk so brazen. He accused him of being wicked whose vicious advice would plunge the Kuru empire in abysmal depths. Vidhur patiently assimilated everyone's viewpoint. He had faith in Bhishma and Drona's integrity. They were the two pillars of the empire who always had its welfare in mind. Their quest for truth and honesty vouched for their credibility. None of their decisions were driven by self gratifying interests. Anyone who cast aspersions on their intentions was likely of evil disposition. He reiterated that Karna's lineage and varna represented his thought process.

VIDHUR LASHES OUT AT DHRITRASHTRA

Vidhur reprimanded Dhritrashtra. He advised him to be righteous and consider Pandu's sons as his own. Bhishma and Drona were the ones with impeccable character and would never injure one in favour of another. Their decisions were unbiased and always for the welfare of all individuals. Vidhur derided Dhritrashtra for his foolishness. Yudhisthira and his brothers were skilful and righteous and would be an asset for the kingdom. Their cousins Vasudev Krishna was their advisor and the brave Balaram was on their side. Drupada, their father-in-law was an influential king.

Vidhura was yet not done with Dhritrashtra. He reproached him for the dishonour Duryodhan's act of conniving with Purochana to kill Pandavs had brought to the royal Bharata lineage. The best way to condone for the evil and rise to the occasion was to give Pandu's sons their due share in the kingdom. An ideal way to end a dispute is through reconciliation. If this were to fail, war would never ever help to achieve the goal unless it was predestined. Duryodhan, Shakuni and Karna were young and foolish. Their immaturity and envy would bring the great dynasty to dust. Moreover by accepting Pandavs they would get their greatest rival Drupada as an ally and also the scion of Yadava dynasty Vasudev Krishna who was invincible.

Tongue lashing from the calm and complacent Vidura embarrassed Dhritrashtra. He was left with no choice but to summon the Pandavs along with their mother and wife from Panchala. Vidura was sent as an emissary. Everyone including Drupada and Pandavs greeted their Vidhura warmly. Vasudeva was hugged fondly.

Vidhur expressed immense pleasure at the matrimonial alliance of his nephews with Draupadi. He extended an invitation on behalf of Dhritrashtra expressing his desire to take the boys back to Hastinapur. He sought Drupada's permission to take away his guests back home.

CHAPTER FIFTEEN
Rajya Labha

Drupada felt it inappropriate to ask his guests to leave. But it was time Yudhisthira along with his brothers went back to Hastinapur and reclaimed his legacy, he opined. He consulted Vasudev Krishna for whom he had high regards. All the wise ones got in a huddle and came to the conclusion, that what was best for the boys. The residents of Hastinapur welcomed sons of Pandu. Duryodhan and his brothers were full of malice and anger. Dhritrashtra was left with no option but to abide by the commands of Vidhur, Drona and Bhishma. Duryodhan's evil acts had brought him and the kingdom tremendous shame. Once the damage is done it cannot be undone but he tried to make amends to prevent from being further ridiculed.

YUDHISTHIRA GETS KHANDVAPRASTHA

Soon after Dhritrashtra called upon Yudhisthira and gave him the far flung half of the kingdom, that was a raw deserted forest, Khandvaprastha. With this apparent righteous but crafty act he hoped to keep his sons away from their cousins without causing much embarrassment to him. He wanted to establish himself as a just king, erasing the image of a father who was more inclined towards his sons to the extent of forging his own brother's sons rights to inheritance. Without questioning Yudhisthira accepted whatever their uncle offered and left for Khandvaprastha with Vasudev in tow as their philosopher and guide.

Under Vasudev's expert guidance a beautiful city came up. It was well planned. The entire land was measured and a whole plan was worked on it for a township. For protection it was surrounded by a huge moat and a high wall was erected. There were double gates at the entrance. The turrets were well stocked beyond the imagination of the enemy, full of varied weapons that could kill hundreds of enemies in one shot. Khandvaprastha now had huge mansions adorning it. It came to be known as the city of Indraprastha. It was now the official residence and kingdom of Pandavs. Indraprastha was no longer dry and deserted. It was full of beautiful gardens loaded with beautiful plantation and trees, house to wild animals and beautiful birds. Besides Brahmins and kshatriyas who resided here trade too flourished. Artisans and merchants producing varied crafts flourished. Having helped Kunti and Yudhisthira settle Vasudev Krishna along with his brothers bid farewell and left for Dvaravati.

CHAPTER SIXTEEN
Arjuna Vanavasa Parva

Pandu's sons transformed the arid jungle Khandvaprastha with the help of his cousin Vasudev Krishna into heaven Indraprastha. The past was now just a shadow, all forgotten and erased but enriched with experience. Yudhisthira ruled with benevolence. He abided by the law. The citizens were overtly happy with him. They had lots of respect for their king. Draupadi maintained a harmonious relationship amongst all. All the of them with their wife and mother lived like one big happy family.

The great scholar Narada, came to pay a visit to the Kuru heirs. The brothers in unison paid obeisance to the great Brahmin. Draupadi too joined to seek blessings. Narada, expressed his reservations about the relationship equation changing in due course of time between the brothers with the presence of a woman in their life. Common interests in life can do irreparable damage at times.

SUNDA AND UPSUNDA

Narada recounted the tale of two brothers' Sunda and Upasunda. Both of them were brave, valorous and invincible. Right from childhood there was lots of love and comradeship between the two. Each excelled the other and vice versa. There was no soul who could make one stand up against the other. Once they reached of age, both left the comfort and confines of home and moved to the mountains to practise austerities, learn the Vedas and art of warfare. Tough life left them all rags and bones. But with every passing day they were enriched, wiser, skilful and humble.

Even Brahma got envious of their strength of mind and body. After the great rise comes the great fall. Illusion provided lots of temptations. There were beautiful women all over vying for their attention, feigning to be in trouble to take them away from their path and architect their fall. But all Sunda and Upsunda did was to fold their hands humbly and beg for freedom from temptations. Even the self created universe had no choice but to grant them the boon. Both of them had toiled hard to reach the zenith and attain fame on earth among men. But would they be immortal, always in the hearts and minds of others! Well no! Their aim in life was to be the most powerful among humans lest no one would defeat them.

Having attained the boon of invincibility they set aside their austere ways of life. Hard work was replaced by enjoyment and pleasure. There was no danger they could not counter. They were invincible, at least from any physical attack. The only people who could defeat them without weapons were the Brahmins. Mad with envy, without any rational they began killing the Brahmins. All of them out of fear for their lives started going into hiding. Unfortunately they were tracked, hunted and killed.

A total state of chaos descended on the once happy peaceful State. Afraid of being defeated, Sunda and Upsunda unleashed a reign of terror. People stopped celebrating festivals. The land was now arid, bare and devoid of happiness. The once humble beings had become demons, detested and feared by all. With all the Brahmins defeated and subdued, there was not a soul left in the kingdom who would dare to confront them. After darkness, there is light. Brahma has its own way of establishing justice.

Both the brothers were smitten by Tilotamma, an exquisite beauty. She was both noble and wise. Consumed with desire both wished to marry, irrespective of her consent. None asked as to whom she would want to wed! The brothers started fighting. Mortified, Tilotamma just stood rooted, on looking the horrific spectacle. Each wanted the other to relent and back off. But intoxicated with pride, they could not bring themselves to give up. After a prolonged struggle, almost half dead, both succumbed. Universe blessed Tilotamma, for her strength of character and endurance to withstand evil.

Narada in an extremely subtle fashion explained his point of view. Getting a whiff of Narada's thoughts, Yudhisthira decided to institute a code of conduct, lest Draupadi, became the cause of family's dissemination. Thus it was decided, as to when Draupadi was with one of the brothers in her chamber, others would not enter or even caste a covetous look on her. In case of any transgression it would result in banishment for a period of twelve years.

Indraprastha prospered immensely with the passage of time. Neighbouring kingdoms accepted the sovereignty of Yudhisthira and his brothers. Draupadi took pride in her valorous husbands. She was like goddess Saraswati with her elephants.

Once some thieves stole a brahmin's cow. He was extremely distressed. His only means of sustenance was forcibly taken away by jackals. Under Yudhisthira's righteous rule, Arjun's valour and Bhim's bull like strength, this act was blasphemous. Full of wrath and anger he came knocking. On listening to his plight, Arjun could not think rationally. In haste, he rushed to Draupadi's chamber to fetch his arms. Draupadi was with Yudhisthira. Without giving it a second thought Arjun carried his arms with the Brahmin in tow and set out in search of the thief.

Riding high on his chariot, wearing his armour with a bow and arrow in hand, Arjun rushed, lest the thief left the city and was untraceable. The thief had not reached far enough yet. Once in line of vision, the man was pierced by arrows. The warrior had done his duty. On reaching the city Arjun got a hero's welcome. It is a king's duty to safeguard the interest of his subjects. The mission had been accomplished successfully.

But now a Damocles' sword swung on Yudhisthira's head. The duty of a warrior is to help people in distress. This is his foremost dharma. Accordingly Arjun had not transgressed any law or rule by storming in Draupadi's chamber. But a predetermined law had been violated. Arjun in spite of Yudhisthira's entreaties did not deter from his decision. He on the other hand was adamant. His older brother's love for him was making him go weak. Laws cannot be amended at convenience. He recounted righteous Yudhisthira's very own words to him.

Arjun after full consecration rites, left for the forest, to live the life of a celibate for twelve years. He was accompanied by ascetics and raconteurs. Of course there were Lord Indra and Marut to soothe. It was a pleasure travelling through the forests with meandering lakes and melodious singing of birds. On the way they stopped over at places of pilgrimage. The priests travelling along performed fire sacrifices, asking in turn for blessings. Wonderful stories of valour were narrated, en route. Finally, all of them reached, from where river Ganga had originated. They pitched their tents.

ARJUN MARRIES ULIPI

Life carried on for Arjuna. He spent the days hunting, practising his weapons, performing ablutions and sporting in Ganges water. During one such moment, he had a close encounters with Ulupi, daughter of a Naga king Kouravya. Ulupi was smitten. She was aware that Arjuna was under vow of celibacy. But the youngster was head over heels in love with the handsome warrior. If her love was not reciprocated, she was sure to take her life and die. The thought made Arjuna shudder. He agreed to unite with her lest be burdened by someone's death. This would taint his soul and would be against dharma. Arjun spent time with Ulupi in her father's palace. Finally he took leave.

The Kuru prince now travelled the length and breadth of high mountains, the Vashishitas, mount Mahendra. Riches were distributed among ascetics. They happened to cross over the beautiful forest Naimisha with beautiful river Utpalin. Great rivers Nanda, Upananda, Gaya and Ganga also came on the way. Finally he reached Manalura. Arjun went and paid obeisance to the king Chitravahana.

ARJUN MARRIES CHITRANGADA

Chitrangada was Chitravahana's only child. She was a beauty. In order to continue his lineage, Chitravahana wished to make her his putrika. Accordingly, in keeping with the custom, after marriage the daughter would continue to live in her father's house and the son born to her, would be the king. Besotted by Chitrangada's grace and elegance, Arjun agreed to the king's demands and lived with his daughter in the palace for three winters. He then took leave.

The warrior continued his journey moving towards south. It was full of beautiful oceans and places of pilgrimage. But surprisingly all the places of pilgrimage were desolate, without ascetics. The rumours doing the rounds were that crocodiles infested the oceans and for fear of their life people kept away. The warrior was not the one to be intimidated by wild animals. In his youth he had torn apart a crocodile with his arrows when his preceptor Drona was attacked while others had just stood and gaped.

Fearlessly he went to have a dip in the holy waters of river Soubhadra. While bathing joyfully, he seemed to have got stuck and got pulled inside the base of the ocean. Arjun fought back and dragged the creature out of water with all his might. He was absolutely taken aback. It was a beautiful woman who was bathing in the deep waters. This was extremely intriguing as to why the lady, Varga was harassing poor ascetic pilgrims. Varga on being cornered narrated her ordeal to Arjun.

Once, Varga and her four equally beautiful friends, while frolicking in the forest, came across an ascetic who was deep in meditation. He was so keenly absorbed in his work that he just did not notice them. This offended the girls to no end. They felt insulted. Like Maneka tempting Vishvamitra, they did not give up but instead tried to seduce him. Enraged at their mean behaviour he reprimanded them. The girls felt humiliated. Youth and beauty had made them proud and vain. In their arrogance they had incurred the wrath of a humble man. Unable to face the world all the five spent time at different pilgrimages, now and then hounding ascetics and pilgrims, seeking revenge. Arjun was in a quandary. Varga had realised her folly. She was begging him for forgiveness. People who seek mercy should be redeemed from sin. Moreover killing a woman is against law. Arjun forgave Varga and her friends. The pilgrimages were freed from the curse of the friends. They became holy places for women.

Meanwhile Chitrangada gave birth to Arjun's son king Babhruvahana. She in accordance with law continued to live with her father.

The Pandav now moved towards the west, after seeing his son. He scoured the western shores and reached Prabhasa. Vasudev Krishna too came to pay a visit. Both the intelligent and valiant cousins discussed events and happenings. Krishna approved of the latter's decision of leaving Indraprastha. The two men then moved to mount Raivataka. After spending days on the beautiful hillock, they proceeded to Dvaraka. Both were welcomed wholeheartedly by its people. The Vrishnis, Bhojas, Andhakas, women, children all came to pay homage to the Kuru heir.

CHAPTER SEVENTEEN
Subhadra-Harana Parva

A festival was being celebrated on mount Raivata. Bhojas, Vrishnis and Andhakas along with illustrious ascetics gathered to celebrate. Warriors gave away lots of riches to the latter. There was singing and dancing during celebrations. The place in general was decorated like a beautiful starry night, lit by the full moon. People were dressed in finery and ornaments. Even the chariots were not left bare. Balarama, Vasudev Krishna's brother accompanied by his wife Revati and a group of musicians were in a highly intoxicated state. Ugrasena, king of Vrishnis, was surrounded by his wives. Vasudev accompanied Arjuna since he was the guest of honour. Both of them enjoyed themselves. Arjun was smitten by a young damsel. She happened to be Vasudev's half sister. Subhadra and Vasudev were born of the same father Vasudeva but of different mothers. Sensing his friend's inclination, he proposed to get his sister married to him.

There were no reasons for refusing. Subhadra was a beauty in her own rights. Since she was Vasudev's sister, any grounds for doubting her wisdom and lineage were baseless. Arjun immediately assented. Krishna proposed that he elope with her during the swayamvara. This practice was within the precinct of laws for kshatriyas. Moreover it was best that his sister married Arjuna, who was a brave warrior, of the famous Bharata lineage and son of his aunt Kunti rather than marrying a total stranger. Worst would be that wealth and goods would be given as the bride's price by the groom. It was as though goods were sold and bought. Arjuna agreed.

SUBHADRA IS ABDUCTED

Arjun rushed a messenger to Yudhisthira and Krishna's father Vasudeva. After getting approval he proceeded to accomplish his mission. One day Subhadra along with her friends in tow, left home to enjoy the festivities that were taking place on mount Raivata. A warrior riding high on his chariot, clad in armour, intercepted and dragged her inside his chariot. Both eloped at a breathtaking speed, towards the gates of Dvaraka. Subhadra almost swooned in delight on beholding her handsome, royal abductor.

The guards escorting Subhadra rushed to the assembly hall Sudarma and informed the officiating officer. A bugle was sounded to alert everyone in the city. All the festivities came to a standstill. The Vrishnis, Bhojas and Andhakas gathered, fumed at Arjuna's audacity. Some harped on his ungratefulness. He was a guest and treated with utmost respect. He had acted in an ungracious fashion. Balarama's eyes blazed angrily. All the warriors were ordered to get prepared with their chariots, swords and finger protectors. Arjun had to be tracked, hunted and punished.

Amidst all the commotion, Balarama, now no longer intoxicated realised that his younger brother Vasudev was very quiet and contemplative. He was the wisest of the lot. He thundered at him, "Arjuna came from the famous Kuru lineage, but his behaviour was loathsome. He has disgraced his family's name by forcibly abducting his friend's sister. It was for Krishna's friendship that he was honoured" fumed Balarama. He was now all set and hell bent on taking revenge on the entire Kuru lineage. Balarama was angry at Krishna's fallacy of judgement.

CHAPTER EIGHTEEN
Harana Harika Parva

Vasudev on the contrary had a very different point of view on the entire abduction scenario. Let's not forget that he had orchestrated the entire episode. Arjuna he said was a brave and valorous warrior. There was hardly anyone who could match him in his skills. Moreover, the ethics and values of the famous Bharata lineage were ingrained in him. The famed Kuntibhoja's daughter, Kunti was his mother. He refuted the idea of a swayamvara for his sister Subhadra. In a swayamvara the groom paid the price for the bride which was absolutely demeaning. Moreover in the ceremony, it was not certain whom his younger sister would have ended up choosing and the type of husband he would turn out to be. Arjun was the friend he had known for quite some time and was a noble human being.

ARJUN MARRIES SUBHADRA

As per Krishna's advice the entire family went up to Arjun and expressed remorse at their antagonism. They invited him and Subhadra to stay with them. The brave warrior that the was, it would not have been difficult for Arjun to defeat the entire race of the Yadavs. It was best that he was mollified. It would be disgraceful to be beaten and brought to dust in one's own land. Arjun and Subhadra were married in the presence of family with full honour. The couple stayed back for a year and then moved to Pushkara till the time of Arjun's exile.

Arjuna had been away from his family for very long. As soon as his period of exile was over, he along with Subhadra left for Indraprastha. All the brothers welcomed him and Subhadra fondly.

Draupadi was remorseful at seeing her husband with his new bride. She lamented in grief and anger. Arjun was extremely fond of Draupadi. He wished to appease her and alleviate her suffering. He ordered Subhadra to dress in a humble fashion and take off all the jewels she was wearing. This pacified Draupadi to some extent who in turn hugged her. Both prayed for the glory and fame of their husband.

Once the news of Arjuna having reached Indraprastha reached Dwarka, Subhadra's brothers Krishna and Balarama too followed. They were accompanied by great warriors of Andhaka and Vrishni clan. The brothers came loaded with gifts for Subhhadra and her in laws. Nakul and Sahdev on Yudhisthira's command went to welcome the illustrious ones. In fact the whole city came out to pay homage to the doyens. Krishna and Balarama were pleased at the warm welcome. To the disenchantment of the enemies, the Pandava's treasury overflowed.

All the men gathered, including the hosts and the guests. After initial pleasantries and rituals, they got together to celebrate. There was dancing, music and rounds of drinking bouts. Finally Subhadra's family left except for Vasudev. Krishna and Arjuna spent time discussing and walking along the great Yamuna.

ABHIMANYU IS BORN

Subhadra became mother to a brave and valorous son. He was prone to quick bouts of anger. On account of his temperament, everyone fondly called him Abhimanyu. He was loved by both his paternal as well as maternal uncles. On his birth Yudhisthira donated cows and gold coins to Brahmins. The entire city celebrated his arrival. He was trained to be a great warrior, proficient in the art of handling all weapons, adept in various texts, by his father Arjuna. Both the father and son duo excelled in archery and each gave the other a tough competition. The family was proud to have a son who would instil fear in the minds of enemy.

Draupadi became a mother to five brave sons. Prativindhya was born from Yudhisthira. He had immense knowledge of weapons. Bhimsena became father to Sutasoma. He was a great archer. Arjun had another lion from Draupadi. He was fondly called Shrutakarman. Nakula named his son Shatanika and his twin Sahadev called his, Shrutasena.

Dhouyma presided over and performed all the ceremonies and rituals. As children, their heads were tonsured and all the boys were made to wear sacred threads. Like their fathers, they were also taught Vedas and extensively trained in the use of weapons. It was one big, happy family, very skilful and learned.

CHAPTER NINETEEN
Khandava Daha Parva

On the directives of Dhritrashtra, Yudhisthira along with his brothers continued to live in Indraprastha. They turned the arid and desolate land into a vibrant state. Dharamraj Yudhisthira, the benevolent one, ruled with law as the only yardstick. Being a householder, making wealth and still be righteous, the three diverse entities were synonym to one another under him. The knowledge of varied texts that Dharamraj had acquired all his life, while in Hastinapur and when in anonymity, was practised by him as the king. People of all stratas were treated with utmost respect. All his brothers were equivalent to the four Vedas. There was the rule of law and only law. Where there is justice and fairness, there is no oppression! The chief priest Dhouyma had utmost respect for the king and his brothers. They brought under their control lots of neighbouring kingdoms. Every task was carried out with utmost precision. In general there was an atmosphere of happiness and ease throughout the kingdom.

With the onset of spring season, warm weathers prevailed. Krishna and Arjun along with Draupadi and Subhadra in tow set out to enjoy the waters of Yamuna. Yudhisthira approved of their plans. So all four along with friends left. The women too shed their inhibitions. They danced and sang in an intoxicated state. Expensive and heavy jewels were replaced by bare minimal. The men went frolicking under deep waters.

KHANDAVA IS BURNT

Vasudev and Arjun set out to explore the beautiful wilderness alone on their own. The tract was full of tall trees and birds chirping in the background. After walking miles into the thick forest they seated themselves under the shade of a tree. It felt heavenly as though it was the high seat of their palace designated for the king. Suddenly out of the dense forest appeared a radiant ascetic. Both the Kings among men stood up to pay obeisance.

The ascetic in turn paid rich tributes to them. He was aware that both were brave warriors of illustrious lineages. There was a forest in the vicinity. It was called the Khandava. The ascetic requested the two to help him burn down the Khandava forest. Vasudev and Arjuna were aghast at the suggestion. The ascetic allayed their doubts. Khandava was infested with virulent serpents, wild animals, nagas and gandharvas who attacked the austere, peace loving Brahmins without provocation. Their vileness was offensive. It was time they paid for their sins.

Arjun asked for well bred, swift horses to yoke the chariots. The chariots would have an insurmountable supply of arrows and the bow Gandiva to string, which would match Arjun's strength and skill. Krishna too had come frolicking with Arjun. He too did not have his weapon, the discus. Their demand was accepted.

Arjun mounted the chariot adorned with many flags. He was clad in his armour with finger protectors and a sword slung across his chest. He then lifted the mighty Gandiva and strung it. There were quivers in abundance. Krishna too was equipped with his discus and a vajra in the centre. He also received the club from the Brahmin. Both the warriors now armed with deadly weapons were ready to face humans, animals, nagas, gandharvas and the invisible enemies.

Thus began the great battle where Khandava forest was burnt despite the resistance from Rain and turned to ashes. Arjun and Vasudev stationed themselves on the opposite sides of the forest, mounted on their chariots of supreme energy. The ascetic as bright and energetic as fire himself set the whole forest on fire. In no time the place was engulfed in flames. The fury of fire had its residents scampering in all the eight directions, including the sky and the earth to protect them. The tormentors were now being tormented. It elicited no sympathy and guilt from any quarter. Those who tried to flee the forest were at once torn by either Arjuna's arrows or Krishna's discus. Their target was to not let even a single soul escape.

The ponds in the forest too boiled. The fishes and the crocodiles had never expected to meet such an end. The wailing and sounds of distress echoed in the neighbourhood. It seemed as though a volcano had erupted. A whole ocean of flames could be seen. The survivors waiting for death to overcome desperately prayed to Rain. When summoned, the Lord looked down aghast and poured its blessing in abundance angrily. But it appeared Fire was having a field day. The downpour evaporated midway causing clouds in the sky. In all helplessness Rain watched from above.

The once beautiful forest nurtured by Rain was burnt down. To salvage what was left of it, slayer of Namuchi, poured heavily and angrily at the first opportune moment. At the first stroke of luck a few surviving Nagas and serpents managed to escape. Takshaka's son Ashvasena escaped. Arjun was upset at the deception created by Rain. Some vile creatures were managing to flee. To add to their misery, wild winds blew, heavy clouds hovered churning the ocean. But the warriors' heartfelt prayers were answered. In no time the sky was all clear and the flames of the forest again raged. But unfortunately many birds of Suparna's lineage with sharp claws and beaks started flying overhead and attacking. Some gandharvas, asuras and serpents managed to escape in spite of the fury of clubs and discus. Indra again started its downpour.

At the first opportune moment all the enemies united and charged in unison. But Arjun and Vasudev stood immobile with their respective weapons in hand, ready to face the mob and be victorious. Indra was fascinated by their prowess. But the challenges and odds were still not over. The mountains surrounding the forest started to disintegrate and uproot. Loose rocks and huge trunks of trees came rolling down in fury. The inhabitants of the forest who had managed to escape the fire and Arjun's missiles finally licked dust. But goodness is always protected by destiny. Krishna and Arjun escaped unhurt. The remaining on witnessing the two strong warriors with their weapons that never missed the designated target, combined with the fury of fire and shower of rocks and stones from all sides decided to give up and ran for their life unnoticed.

The annihilation of Khandava was destined. Krishna and Arjun now roamed freely in the forest burning down the rest. Maya, Namuchi's brother was caught, trying to escape. On seeing Krishna's discus and Arjun's arrow aimed at him he cried out in fright. He begged for mercy. Never attack someone who comes begging for refuge! Arjun assured him his safety. Krishna did not want his friend's words negated. He too relented and forgave. Ultimately Maya, Naga king Takshaka's son Ashvasena and four Sharngakas survived the ordeal.

SAGE MANDAPALA AND SHARNGAKA BIRDS

Mandapala lived in the Khandava forest. He was well versed in varied texts. Asceticism was his way of life which he abided by to the hilt. But in spite of his sacrifices and knowledge, he felt incomplete. After much retrospection he realised that that a man needed children to complete him and give happiness which no other accomplishment could bring. Old age is akin to hell without children around. At this ripe old age finding a partner who would beget him children would be impossible. So per functionary he married a Sharngaka bird, Jarita, who gave birth to four children. Now he was a father. His ultimate calling of life too had been fulfilled. In olden times people married trees and birds to ward off evil. This practice is still followed, keeping in mind some superstitious notions.

After performing the rituals of marriage to the Sharngaka bird, Mandapala forgot all about it and carried on life with his wife Lapita and practising austerities. Working hard in good times deprives us of the pain that corrodes in bad times. Jarita and her birds sensed Mandapala's indifferent behaviour. They felt abandoned. But the mother made up for everything that was lacking in their life.

When Khandava was set on fire the mother flapped her wings in helplessness. Her children who had still not developed wings and feet would not be able to fly. The thought that they would be burnt to death in the fire tormented her. She would never abandon them like their father Mandapala but rather die with them. But her wise little children urged her to fly away to a safe place and let destiny protect them. If she were to die in the fire, there would be no further progenies and their lineage would come to an end.

Jarita wished to hide them in a hole made by a rat, in a tree, on which they all lived. The rat had been captured by a hawk. But the children refused. They were not sure whether there were more rats hiding in the hole. It was better to die at the hands of the almighty Fire, than those of a rat. Moreover, their mother in her current state of mind was not able to think rationally and was liable to err.

Jarita flew away to a safe place agonising over the fate of her children. In the meantime, Mandapala on witnessing the forest flames, almost passed out in grief. His children were in the forest, alone and helpless, while he had been careless and negligent. Like a man possessed he set out in search of Jarita and the children. His wife Lapita provoked him into coming with her and escaping the fire. She accused him of loving Sharngaka and the children more than her. For once Mandapala refused to listen. He prayed fervently to Agni to protect his young ones. Even Agni would not turn down the request of the austere frugal ascetic.

After Vasudev Krishna and Arjun had burnt down the forest, the birds miraculously came out unscathed. Jarita was overwhelmed on seeing her children alive. Mandapala too in the meantime came searching for them though his wife Lapita was furious at his devotion. On the other hand Jarita and her children turned away on seeing Mandapala. He had deceived them. The father too had grouses. He had prayed relentlessly for their well being. He had cared more for them than for his wife Lapita. Feeling of insecurity and jealousy drives people to irrational thinking. This clouds their radiance to some extent. Jarita and her children relented.

Mandapala escorted all the birds out of the forest. In the meantime, the entire forest was engulfed in flames. After a tough fight and hard work Maya, Krishna and Arjun walked away from the forest now all dust and ashes. Arjuna thanked Universe for the help it had rendered and for the success of the mission. He prayed, for even more weapons that were absolutely divine and extremely lethal. Vasudev Krishna too thanked the Almighty. He asked for nothing else but for the eternal friendship and love of Arjun.

CHAPTER TWENTY
Sabha Parva

Maya accompanied Vasudev and Arjuna on their way back home. He was no longer the demon but a man humbled by circumstances and benevolence of his apparent executioner. Maya in turn wished to pay back for the gratitude bestowed on him. Krishna did not want anything for himself. But to let Maya feel at an equal footing he asked him to build an assembly hall for the Pandavs. The demon belonged to the class of Vishvakarmas. They were excellent craftsmen. An assembly hall in the form of an aircraft, befitting Yudhisthira's stature would be an excellent pay back gift! Krishna instructed the demon to put in all his architectural skills to make it a world class structure.

ASSEMBLY HALL

Thus being accepted into the family of Pandavs and endorsed by Yudhisthira, the work on the most opulent structure took off. At the initiation of the auspicious event, thousands of Brahmins were offered food and sweets. Then the piece of land on which the structure would come up was duly measured. The work on the magnificent hall began.

Maya sought permission from Yudhisthira to travel north of mount Kailasha, where the beautiful lake Bindu rested. The bed of the lake was full of beautiful precious stones. The demon king Vrishaparva ruled there. Maya had placed a magnificent club in the custody of the king. Then there was also a conch shell Devadatta, with an amazing echo. The demon was confident that the king being an honest man would give all his possessions back. Maya with Vrishaparva's permission brought back all the treasure with the help of demons.

Once back, he again set out to work on the hall. He handed over the club to Bhim and the conch shell to Arjuna. All the precious stones were studded in the hall. The highlight was the pond in which he had exquisitely carved out lotuses with precious stones. When filled with clear water it appeared to be in continuation with the rest of the floor. The assembly hall built was befitting Yudhisthira's royal stature and skill. It had beautiful tall pillars, exquisitely carved out in gold. Roughly eight thousand demons were employed to guard the palace.

After a toil of nearly fourteen months, the assembly hall finally stood ground, all regal. A day was anointed when it would be officially inaugurated. All the kings of neighbouring states were invited. Before that thousands of Brahmins were duly fed, given clothes and valuables. Rajrishi Dhouyma was given a place of honour in the hall along with kings and brave warriors. Yudhisthira along with his brothers adorned the five royal seats.

The scholar rishi Narada, who at that point of time was touring the earth, was also invited. He came with his entourage of fellow Brahmins. He was received with utmost respect by Yudhisthira. Narada wished to know about the state of affairs of Indraprastha. After exchanging pleasantries he questioned Yudhisthira on his mode of governance. Narada with his wisdom imparted all the knowledge required for efficient governance. He questioned Yudhisthira.

NARADA ADVISES YUDHISTHIRA

Whether he enjoyed his duties or felt burdened by them! Hope he was not compromising on good values and ethics to earn wealth and subjugate neighbouring kingdoms! Fulfilling desires are important but not at the cost of duties and laws. All the three have to work in sync.

It is not the king alone who has to be intelligent. He cannot function all by himself. He needs a team that is equally efficient. The chief officers assisting him should be faithful and devoted to their job. A king's decision should be based on information he receives from his messengers and advisors. Rise and fall of a kingdom depends on wise counsel but kept in folds from others by the advisor. It is foolish to seek counsel from every known person or rely on just one. But then a single intelligent, learned, sincere one would be enough to take the kingdom to nadir.

A king who is lazy and does not act appropriately on the counsel of his advisors loses out on precious time and is bound not to prosper. Even the princes, young and old, officials, warriors should be counselled by learned Brahmins. There needs to be a strong network of spies, who work independently to unearth conspiracies within and in the neighbourhood.

Money from the exchequer ought to be used prudently and not wasted on luxury. When an enemy is attacked there are roads that lead to justice. It can be negotiations and bribery. If the former does not work it could be punishment and discord. But good decision making would come from having advisors well versed in texts of high order that teach good governance. And foremost would be their honesty and of their families over generations.

A kingdom and its subjects would be happy when the granaries overflow with food grain and the treasury with cash. The soldiers too need to be equipped with armour and weapons, and their families taken care off in their absence or when killed while fighting for the state. Only the king's achievements should do the rounds among his people and not what he intended to achieve and could not.

In general the officials, be it the chief advisor or others ought to be treated with respect by the king. They are the backbone of an effectual governance. The ministers should not be at liberty to treat the subjects harshly without the knowledge of the head. Wages and ration not given on time, to employees would cause a major upheaval in an empire. But a reward for any achievement big or small helps cultivate faithful comrades.

It is not only unwise but rather foolish to attack without preparedness. The army should be well equipped with elephants, cavalry, infantry, chariots, charioteers and above all servants, allies and spies. Preparedness is the key to winning a battle. Even the vassals of the defeated territory should be protected and treated with respect. To motivate and express gratitude for good work accomplished by the heads of the army, they should be given a part of the valuables received.

A disloyal servant engaged in any service would prove to be lethal. Choosing loyal people in the services and protecting them from others becomes important. The first half of the day needs to be essentially used for work, revenue collection, maintaining accounts and so on. The latter half could be engaged in merry making. In case of a famine or any other calamity, the farmers look forward to the king for subsidised loans.

Above all, being impartial is one trait, the head of the state must be endowed with. He is Yama, lord of justice incarnate for his subjects. The five officers who look after the city, the palace, the countryside, the treasury and law ought to work in coordination and be brave, wise and honest. The king's physician should be a man endowed with knowledge of human physiology and have the king's interest at heart.

The most important and foremost is mental peace. Looking after the welfare of ageing and ailing gives an immense sense of purpose to life. Narada asked whether Yudhisthira paid obeisance to Brahmins and offered them food at regular intervals out of reverence. Besides, a king's good conduct is reflected in his knowledge and study of higher texts.

The birth of children reflects the success of the sacred institution. Maintaining of holy fire though symbolic reflects the head of state's leaning and his grinding in Vedas. He hoped no innocent was put to death because of the corrupt officials indulging in bribery.

Traders coming from faraway lands ought not to be fleeced but only appropriately taxed, said Narada. Only a minimal fixed tax needed to be implemented. On home turf too, for effective results, all artisans ought to be supplied with raw material, wages and tools, four months in advance. Besides the holy texts, commented Narada, the study of science of arms, architecture and different fields must be made mandatory.

Finally, it was the Brahma's justice that punished the evil and wrong doers. The king is the father to all, the infirm, the old and helpless or the orphan. Yudhisthira bowed to the illustrious one and thanked him. The parting shot from the sage was to look after all the four stratas of society for attaining the respect of the whole kingdom.

Like a competitive school boy Yudhisthira wished to know if there was another assembly hall that excelled his. Narada assured him that there was none. At least on earth his was the most regal. God Shakra's in heaven moved from place to place and was a source of eternal peace, happiness, dispelled old age and misery. His wife Shachi, an embodiment of goddess Lakshmi and Sri occupies the seat next to him. It is illuminated by the brilliance of sun. The red bands that appear in the sky represent Shakra's feminine side, modesty and radiance. He is worshipped by the powerful Maruts. The seven great sages, the saptarshis too pay homage.

In Yama's sabha there is no sorrow, hunger and misery. In his abode there are no rivalries or rivals. Men here are free from the cycle of time and lie in cremation grounds on grass, paying homage to Agni. It is the home to both evil and good.

Lord Varuna's sabha is known as Pushkaramalini. The great oceans, rivers, wells, springs and water bodies created by Brahma embody the great god Varuna. All the serpents, churn its waters with their strength. It is their abode. Varuna's bed is endowed with precious stones and beautiful vegetation.

In Kubera's assembly hall the king is dressed in lustrous attire and precious jewels. He is surrounded by women all the time. There are gandharvas and apsaras singing and dancing. The audience are most of the time gorging on flesh of animals and possessing terrible weapons. The alliance of the king and god Kubera, the granter of riches, never ceases.

The sabha of Aditya, the sun god, is absolutely radiant, very energetic and without lethargy. Brahma sits here and creates energy, wind, water, moon, constellations, the Vedas and histories.

Narada, narrated to the brothers the episode of coronation ceremony performed by Harishchandra, who had conquered many islands, establishing power over the entire earth. Harishchandra had commanded all the kings to bring in riches which he distributed generously among the Brahmins. He prodded Yudhisthira to follow the great king's footsteps. The only people who could be an impediment would be the demons born as Brahmins. It was important to insulate against such people who could conjure a war leading to the destruction of earth.

www.ingramcontent.com/pod-product-compliance
Lightning Source LLC
Chambersburg PA
CBHW070122260626
47160CB00004B/1581